FORGIVE the TRESPASSERS

ENDORSEMENTS

A well-written prologue sets the stage for this intriguing novel where the consequences of past behavior have altered the lives of four people. Plenty of guilt abounds, along with blame placed without knowing all the facts. The author's use of tension and splendid imagery will keep the reader turning pages. I highly recommend this story of enduring love and sought-after forgiveness.

—Jo Huddleston, author of the Caney Creek series and *Tidewater Summer*.

Vickie's story of consequences, danger, and forgiveness will draw the reader into the world of Jake Reynolds, his former high school sweetheart, and his best friend. This intriguing page-turner finds Jake returning to his hometown where he must face past and present troubles before finding God's peace and forgiveness. Jake's tale will touch hearts while providing a touch of romance, mystery, and drama. It is well-written and heart-warming.

—Bettie Boswell, author of *On Cue* and contributing author of "From the Lake to the River": Buckeye Christian Fiction Anthology.

Vickie Phelps has woven an intriguing story of a man with a mission who comes "home" after twenty-five years and finds himself caught up in of trouble. I was drawn into the story from the very first page and it did not disappoint through all the twists and turns. Vickie's writing flows well and draws you into the lives of the characters through colorful descriptions, dialogue, and glimpses into their thoughts. I'll be making sure my friends know about this excellent book.

—**Shirley Crowder**, Christian author and speaker

Vickie Phelps' new book has it all...engaging characters, a dramatic backstory, and a message of hope and forgiveness that any reader will love.

—**Cheryl Wray**, Coordinator of Southern Christian Writers Conference

FORGIVE the TRESPASSERS

VICKIE PHELPS

ELK LAKE PUBLISHING INC.

PUBLISHING THE POSITIVE
Plymouth, Massachusetts

COPYRIGHT NOTICE

Cover and Interior Design: Derinda Babcock
Editor(s): Mary Johnson, Deb Haggerty
PUBLISHED BY: Elk Lake Publishing, Inc., 35 Dogwood Drive, Plymouth, MA 02360, 2021

LIBRARY CATALOGING DATA

Names: Phelps, Vickie (Vickie Phelps)
Forgive the Trespassers / Vickie Phelps
252 p. 23cm × 15cm (9in × 6 in.)
ISBN-13: 978-1-64949-382-8 (paperback) | 978-1-64949-383-5 (trade paperback) | 978-1-64949-384-2 (e-book)
Key Words: forgiveness; betrayal; broken promises; sins of the past; bitterness; change of heart; love triangle; Texas romance
Library of Congress Control Number: 2021946753 Fiction

ACKNOWLEDGMENTS

Thank you to Deb Haggerty and the staff at Elk Lake Publishing for bringing *Forgive the Trespassers* to life. I had almost given up on the book, then you gave the story a chance. I'm forever grateful. A special thanks to my editor, Mary Johnson, for her patience and expertise as we worked through the pages. The work was worth it.

A special thank you to Jessica Ferguson, Danyce Gustafson, Kassy Paris and Amber Tinsley for reading an early draft of this book and giving me honest, helpful critiques. Ladies, your suggestions and remarks helped make this a better book. I'm in your debt for reading through all those pages and taking the time to help me get the story right.

As always, thank you, Sonny, for allowing me to spend time doing what I love.

To God be the glory, great things he has done.

PROLOGUE

JUNE 5, 1957

Jake's heart twisted into a knot as a single tear rolled down Marilyn's face and dripped onto the front of her pink cotton blouse.

"Please don't leave," she whispered.

He slipped his arm around her and pulled her close.

The words of "Only You," by The Platters, echoed through Malone's Burger Shack. Jake and Marilyn had adopted the song as theirs.

"I'll be back before you know it," he said. "Three months isn't forever. The summer will be over in no time."

Movement nearby caught Jake's attention. Carl Malone finished clearing the table next to theirs and looked at Jake. The slender, middle-aged café owner wiped his hands on a towel slung across his shoulder. "You kids need anything else? I'm gonna be closing up here pretty soon."

Jake shook his head.

"No, sir, thank you."

Mr. Malone started to walk away.

"Sir?"

Carl looked back. "Yeah?"

"Thank you for letting us spend the evening here and play the same song on the jukebox so many times."

Malone winked. "It's okay. Believe it or not, I was your age once. I remember what it was like to spend time with someone special." He walked off, a smile crinkling the corners of his mouth.

Jake turned to Marilyn. "Guess we better get going."

She nodded but didn't say anything. He knew she was upset about his leaving, but no one hated it any more than he did. They'd graduated from Archer Springs High last month, but he hadn't been able to find even part-time employment. Archer Springs was a small town, and most people who lived in the area were farmers. Jake had almost given up hope of finding work, and then two days ago, harvesters had come through on their way north to work the crops. When word got around that they needed workers, Jake applied.

Outside, Jake led Marilyn to the turquoise and white '57 Chevy in the parking lot. It belonged to Dale Summers, his best friend. The car had been a graduation present to Dale from his folks, with less than a thousand miles on the odometer. Dale had offered it to him for his last night in town.

Jake opened the driver's side door, and Marilyn climbed in, scooting across the seat to make room for him. Three miles out of town, Jake pulled into Pearce's Lookout and parked under a large sweet gum tree. He glanced around and saw they had the place to themselves. An easy breeze wandered in through the open window, and the sound of cicadas filled the night air. Jake reached under the seat and pulled the lever, moving the seat for more room.

He leaned back against the door to face Marilyn. When he pulled her into his arms, she pressed her face against his chest, her body trembling with silent sobs.

"Shhh. Don't cry." He gently kissed her wet face, his lips lingering near the corner of her mouth.

"Jake, I can't stand the thought of you being gone all summer."

"Am I worth waiting for?" He hoped his joking would make her smile.

She sniffed and wiped at her face with her hand. "I'm ready for us to be together. I can't wait to get out of the house. You know how Daddy is. Nothing pleases him."

Jake nodded. "I know, sweetheart, but it won't be for long. Can you hold out for three more months?" He rubbed her back gently, trying to comfort her. He kissed the top of her head. "You didn't answer my question. Am I worth waiting for?"

She raised her head and looked at him, tears brimming in her hazel eyes. "Jake Reynolds, what kind of question is that?"

He grinned.

"Just checking." He reached for a small box on the dashboard and held it out. "For you."

She straightened, took the box, and lifted the lid. One half of a gold heart dangled from a delicate gold chain. Jake reached inside his pocket and pulled out a matching half.

"I'll keep this half with me. He took the chain and pressed the two halves together, making a whole heart. "There's a message written on it. Together we are one heart."

Marilyn smiled and nodded. "Yes, we are. One heart. Soulmates."

He slipped his half of the heart back into his pocket and placed the chain around her neck. It glowed in the moonlight against her creamy skin. "Something to remember me by."

Marilyn closed her hand around the heart. "It's wonderful, but I could never forget you." She released her hold on the pendant. Cupping his face with her hands, she brushed her lips across his. "I'll always love you. I promise I'll wait if it takes forever."

Jake stared at her for a moment.

"You're so beautiful."

Before she could respond, he kissed her. Her arms slipped around his neck, and she leaned against him. As she continued to kiss him, Jake felt himself losing control. Somewhere in the back of his mind, he could hear his grandfather's voice.

Jake, don't ever let your emotions override common sense. You'll be sorry if you do.

He reached up and pulled the ribbon from Marilyn's ponytail. Her long brown hair fell around her shoulders in a silky veil to surround her face. He buried his hands in it. The smell of the lavender scent she wore floated around them, timeless, sweet, seductive.

His grandfather's words faded in and out of his consciousness like a radio station interrupted by a stronger frequency. It wasn't the way they'd expected to seal their love, but there'd never been anyone else for either of them. There never would be. They were already wedded to each other in their hearts.

God would forgive them this one time, wouldn't he?

Marilyn opened the front door and slipped inside. The dark house indicated her parents had gone to bed.

"Is that you, Marilyn?" Her mother's soft voice came from the direction of the sofa.

Marilyn couldn't see her face, but her mother's slender form stood and walked toward her.

"Yes, Mother."

"Out kind of late, aren't you? You know your daddy would be upset if he was awake."

"Yes, ma'am."

"You and Jake must have had a lot to talk about."

Marilyn sighed. "He's leaving in the morning. It was our last night together for three months."

Her mother's arm slipped around her shoulders. "I'm sorry. I know it will be a long summer for you, but he'll be back before you know it." She reached up to stroke her daughter's hair. "I thought you wore your hair pulled back tonight. You asked me for some ribbon."

Marilyn remembered Jake pulling it from her hair, but everything had happened so fast, she had forgotten to redo the ponytail. What had happened to the piece of pink satin? Her heart thumped against her chest, waiting for her mother to question her. She reached up and touched her hair.

"I must have lost it somewhere."

"How could you lose it and not know?"

Marilyn's mouth was dry. "I've been so upset with Jake leaving I haven't even thought about the ribbon." A thin finger of guilt tapped her on the chest, and she cringed, glad her mother couldn't see her face. She hadn't remembered the ribbon until her mother mentioned it.

Her mother hugged her, then pulled back. "Marilyn, you're trembling. What's wrong, honey? You and Jake didn't have a disagreement, did you?"

Tears stung Marilyn's eyes. "No. I just don't want him to leave."

"I know. Sometimes we face things in life that don't seem fair." She patted her daughter's arm. "You'd better go get some sleep. You'll feel better in the morning."

Marilyn went to her room and closed the door. As she undressed and slipped into her nightgown, she thought about the evening she'd spent with Jake. She hoped her mother was right. Maybe time would pass quickly and he would come home. A thought flashed through her mind. What if he didn't? A cold chill ran over her. She shivered, climbed into bed, and pulled the sheet up to her chin. She clasped her half of the gold heart in her hand. Jake had promised, and she was counting on it.

Jake pulled into Dale Summers's driveway and parked the '57 Chevy. He sat there for a moment, savoring the time he'd spent with his girl. The fact he had to leave the next day was the only smudge on an almost perfect evening. His chest tightened. He regretted what had happened, but no one would be the wiser. They'd soon be man and wife.

The porch light blinked on, and Dale stepped outside. Jake watched him walk toward the car with the familiar Summers swagger. Dale was a good three inches shorter than he, and a bit heavier, but his midnight black hair, good looks, and total confidence had won him the award of Most Handsome in their senior class. He could have any girl he wanted. Dale leaned his arms on the car door and grinned at Jake.

"You gonna sit in the car all night?"

Jake opened the door and climbed out. He handed Dale the keys. "Thank you for letting me use the car." He patted the hood of the Chevy and ran his hand down the vehicle's sleek contoured fender.

"You can use it any time you need to." Dale pocketed the keys, and then bent to retrieve something from the ground beneath the car door. He held up the satin ribbon from Marilyn's hair and grinned again. "You and Marilyn have a good time?"

Jake snatched the ribbon, stuffing it in his shirt pocket. "The best, thanks to you."

"It's going to be awful boring around here this summer with you gone."

Jake swallowed hard and tried not to think about the next three months. "Oh, I'm sure you'll find something to do." He slapped his friend on the shoulder. "Every girl in town wants a ride in this car."

"What fun is it if your best friend isn't here to go along?"

Jake sighed. "You'll still have Kay to go out with."

Dale kicked the front tire with the toe of his shoe. "I know, but the four of us have been together for so long, it doesn't seem right that one of us is leaving." He squinted at his friend. "How's Marilyn taking it?"

"Not good." A lump formed in Jake's throat. Leaving would be harder than he'd thought.

Dale shoved his hands into his jeans pockets. "My old man would probably loan you some money to get you started." He tilted his head and regarded Jake for a moment. "He thinks a lot of you. I'll ask him if you want me to."

Jake shook his head. "Thanks for the offer, but I need to earn the money myself. We can't start life together on someone else's money."

"Okay, but you know who to call if you ever need help." Dale pulled the keys from his pocket. "Come on, I'll drive you home."

They climbed into the car and Dale backed out of the driveway. The two boys were silent as they made their way to Jake's house. They had discussed his leaving several times over the past few days.

Jake's chest felt as though a concrete block had been tied around it. When Dale stopped in front of the house, he turned to his friend. "Do me a favor, would you?"

"Sure, anything you want."

"Keep an eye on Marilyn for me. I feel bad about leaving her for the whole summer."

Dale nodded. "You bet. Don't worry. She can go places with me and Kay whenever she wants to. That way, she won't be sitting at home by herself all the time. We'll look after her."

"Thanks." They shook hands, and Jake stepped out of the car.

Dale leaned over and looked out the window. "I'll take good care of Marilyn. You can count on it."

CHAPTER 1

SUNDAY, JUNE 6, 1982

Jake Reynolds had vowed never to set foot in Texas again, specifically in Archer Springs. And he hadn't, until today. This place reeked of bad memories, and coming back would only resurrect them.

He drove the streets, reliving his childhood, as he passed familiar landmarks. It didn't take him long. The town looked even smaller than he remembered, or maybe he had been living in a big city for too long. He turned around at the city limits sign and drove back toward the center of town. He took a left onto Orchard Street. No sense in putting it off any longer.

He pulled his red Chevy truck to a stop at the house that had belonged to Uncle George and Aunt Nora. His breath caught in his throat as he looked at the crumbling structure in front of him. Regret surged through his chest. It was the oldest part of town, and most of the houses were in varying degrees of decay. At one time, these had been nice homes, not expensive, but well taken care of, their owners respected. Now most of them stood empty. The few who were occupied looked like a strong wind might carry them away for good.

He turned his attention to the house he had inherited. Broken windowpanes stared at him like skeletons' eyes.

The once-white paint hung in brittle curls from years in the blazing Texas sun. The screen door swung on one hinge.

He opened the door of the pickup and stepped out, stretching his six-foot-one frame. His muscles felt stiff after the drive from Georgia to Texas. He walked around the truck a couple of times to get the kinks out, then turned to face the house again. An involuntary groan erupted from deep inside him, and he rubbed his hands across his eyes in an attempt to block out the decay before him. He dreaded what awaited him inside.

Jake opened the gate and waded through the knee-high weeds in the yard, their dry blades swishing against his jeans as though in protest at being disturbed. He tested the sagging porch step with one foot and decided it would hold his weight.

As he walked toward the door, he gazed at the old porch swing dangling on a rusty chain. It seemed like only yesterday he and Aunt Nora had sat in that swing, sipping iced tea and eating fresh-baked pound cake. He could almost hear their voices.

"Aunt Nora, guess what?"

"My goodness, Jake, what's got you so excited?" She smiled. "It must have something to do with Marilyn."

He grabbed Aunt Nora, pulled her to her feet, and danced her around. "She said yes, Aunt Nora. Marilyn said yes. She's promised to marry me."

Aunt Nora laughed and hugged him.

"This calls for a celebration," she said. "You get the iced tea, and I'll get the cake. Let's go sit in the swing and talk about this promise you two made."

Jake shook his head at the memory. Those days were gone. Aunt Nora had died from a massive heart attack the year after he left Archer Springs. And Marilyn's promise? Dead too. The difference was her promise wouldn't stay buried. Even after twenty-five years, it kept resurrecting itself at unsuspecting moments.

Jake pulled on the screen door and the remaining rusty hinge gave way. He leaned the door against the wall and turned the knob on the main door. It opened without any problem, and he stepped inside. So much for locks. Of course, no one had been here to take care of the house, so it had been broken into long ago. Cans and bottles littered the floor. He kicked the debris out of his path as he walked, stirring up dust which clung to his boots and jeans. An old sofa in one corner sported so many holes, the upholstery was almost nonexistent.

He made his way toward the kitchen, choking on a smell like rotten produce. Several empty cans on the kitchen counter had mold growing inside them. Jake wrinkled his nose in disgust. Insects had discovered the remaining tidbits of food clinging to the cans and vied for position, buzzing and swarming over the greenish-black foul-smelling feast. Jake opened the back door to let in fresh air.

In one of the bedrooms, an old iron bed frame sporting a ragged mattress stood in the corner beneath a window with broken glass. Someone had been sleeping here. An old blanket and a pillow with no case lay on the bed. They looked newer than anything else in the house. Maybe a transient from the nearby train yard had taken up residence. Whoever it was had at least kept this room free of garbage.

Not so with the bathroom. When Jake opened the door, a nauseating stench rushed toward him. He gagged and staggered backward. The toilet had been used even though it wasn't in working order. The summer heat intensified the putrid smell. Jake held his breath as he rushed to the front door and out onto the porch, gasping for fresh air to breathe.

A man standing at the bottom of the steps peered up at Jake from under a wide-brimmed straw hat, his thumbs hooked around the straps of a well-worn pair of overalls. He had the most piercing blue eyes Jake had ever seen. They looked as though they could see straight through him. Something about them seemed familiar.

The old man pushed his hat further back on his head. "What you lookin' for?"

Jake took another deep breath. "Not looking, exactly. Investigating my property."

The man rocked forward on his feet as if trying to get a closer look at Jake. "You buy this place?"

Jake shook his head. "No, I inherited it from my uncle when he died."

The old man squinted in the afternoon sun, searching Jake's face. "Say, aren't you George and Nora Reynolds' nephew? Jake, is it?"

"Yes, sir."

The older man held out his hand. "I guess you don't remember me. Carl Malone."

Jake took a closer look at the other man. The blue eyes stared back at Jake from beneath bushy white brows, and then a lot of old memories flashed before him. "Mr. Malone from the Burger Shack?"

"Yes, but that old place is gone. I closed it down ten years ago." The old man shook his head. "Too much competition from the Dairy Queen out on the interstate."

Jake shook the older man's hand, which was still extended toward him. "Sorry, I didn't recognize you, Mr. Malone."

"That's okay, son." He grinned. "Time has a way of changing our faces. You've been gone quite a spell. I remember the day you left." He rubbed his whiskery chin. "How many years has it been now, twenty or more?"

Jake looked out across the yard as if trying to remember, although he knew the date all too well. *June 6, 1957.* "Twenty-five years ago today."

"What brings you back now, after all this time, if you don't mind my asking?"

Jake sighed. "A letter from Sheridan Holdings Company. Seems they want to demolish the house."

Malone pulled off his hat and wiped his brow with a handkerchief before answering. Sweat had plastered his thick white hair to his head.

"James Sheridan and his cohorts are tearing down every house they can get their greedy hands on."

Jake frowned. "What's the purpose of destroying all this property?"

Malone shrugged. "They're calling it some kind of renovation project, but I have my suspicions about their plans. So do a lot of other folks in town. The other day I noticed some equipment parked at the old Miller place outside of town." He squinted at Jake again. "I could be wrong, but it looked like some kind of drilling machinery." He shook his head. "Something strange is going on, that's for sure."

"Nobody's put up a fight about it? They could get up a petition, do a little protesting."

"Wouldn't do any good. These old houses in this part of town are falling down. Some of them have been condemned by the city already. If the city hasn't condemned them, Sheridan sees to it they're either torn down or something worse."

"Meaning what?" Jake didn't like the sound of this renovation project.

Malone edged closer to Jake and lowered his voice. "Seems the folks that don't go along with Sheridan get burned out sooner or later."

"He's burning houses?"

The older man nodded.

Jake snorted. "That's arson. He needs to be stopped."

Malone shook his head. "People are too scared to do anything. Besides, most of them are empty so it doesn't matter to most people what happens to them." He patted the rickety porch railing with one gnarled hand. "If you decide to keep this place, you'll have a fight on your hands for sure. You'll have to go through Sheridan and the town council to boot. They're going along with him." He squinted at Jake for a minute. "You and Dale Summers ran together as boys, didn't you?"

The muscles in Jake's neck tightened. "A long time ago."

"He's on the town council. If you decide to put up a fight, you'll have to contend with both him and Sheridan."

Jake had hoped to slip into town, take care of the house, and leave without being noticed by too many people. The memories this place held weren't all good. He should've known better. Archer Springs, Small Town, USA. They all knew each other's business.

Malone shook his head. "Good luck, son. You're going to need it." He turned and walked out to the street, leaving Jake alone on the porch.

Jake stared at Mr. Malone as he disappeared down the street, thinking about what the old man had said. It sounded like something from an old western movie where the bad guy takes over someone else's land or burns him out. Sheridan sounded like a real piece of work. To top it off, Dale Summers was involved with him—the absolute last person on earth he wanted to run into.

Jake gritted his teeth at the thought of seeing him. Dale had been like the brother Jake never had, but everything changed the summer he left to go work with the harvesters, leaving Marilyn in Dale's care. Now he was involved in what ... arson? Fraud? What had happened to Dale that he had slipped so low as to be a part of shady dealings like this?

An image of Marilyn floated through his mind. She was another person he wanted to avoid. He wasn't sure how he'd react if he saw her. Their last night together had been burned into his memory like a cowboy branding a calf, the iron hot and searing. Her long, brown hair and smile were still familiar after all this time. Those hazel eyes always made him melt when she turned them on him full force. Even now, he could feel her arms around his neck and her lips against his. They'd gone too far their last night together. Jake scraped the back of his hand across his mouth to erase the sensation and clear his thoughts of the painful memories.

He looked at the decay around him. This house had been built by Aunt Nora's grandfather. She and Uncle George never had any children, but they claimed Jake as the son they always wanted. They were the kind of parents he had always wished for. His mother had told him—often—that his birth had been a difficult one, and she'd never regained her health afterward. Although she never said as much in words, she blamed him. He'd always felt like an intrusion in his parents' lives.

Jake turned his thoughts back to the house before him. His aunt and uncle had made him promise the house would always stay in the family. He had a firm belief about promises even as a boy. If you made one, you kept it, regardless of circumstances. Maybe the time had come to make good on this promise.

He couldn't let Sheridan destroy it. He had to do right by Aunt Nora and Uncle George. Besides, no one was going to tear down something that belonged to him—not without his permission, anyway. Jake had always felt he had a good reason for staying away, but now he wished he'd come back sooner. He had allowed the anger and pain from the past to keep him from his responsibilities. A letter from Kay Carter, a mutual friend, had only served as the glue on his determination to stay away. The words played through his mind once more like a broken record.

Dear Jake,

I hate to write you with bad news, but I feel you have the right to know. Marilyn and Dale eloped a few days ago. They drove to Austin without telling anyone and found a Justice of the Peace. They're back in Archer Springs now, living with his parents. I'm so angry at the two of them. How could they do this to us?

I'm still in shock. I wanted to spare you any embarrassment by coming back, expecting Marilyn to be waiting for you. In my case, Dale and I didn't have anything between us except a dating friendship, although I thought it might become more someday. What are we going to do?

Kay

The words had seared themselves into his soul. For days he couldn't eat or sleep. He tried without success to get in touch with Marilyn, but her family told him he'd best let her alone since she was married now.

"It's better this way," his own mother had said, when he phoned home. "Forget Marilyn. Go on with your life. After all, she isn't a proper young lady if she'd marry another man behind your back. She probably *had* to get married."

"How am I supposed to get on with my life? She *is* my life. Or was."

"You want a woman who betrays you?" his mother asked. "What are you, a weakling? It's nothing more than a bad case of puppy love. You'll find somebody else."

Aunt Nora's answers came softer but did nothing to ease his raw pain.

"Jake, a promise is a promise, and Marilyn broke hers. I'm sorry, but you've got to accept facts. It's too late for her to take it back. She's married to another man now."

He thought he would never recover from the smothering emotions enveloping him day after day. Somehow, he'd managed to get through his daily routine, but at night, his eyes stared at a darkened room, his heart aching from the betrayal, sleep coming only after exhausting hours of tossing among twisted sheets. When he did sleep, he dreamed of Marilyn—nightmares where he called her name and then woke in a cold sweat. The nightmares had faded after several years, but he could feel the possibility of one happening real soon with his arrival in Archer Springs.

The attractive dark-haired woman behind the desk smiled as Jake entered the lobby of the Archer Springs Motel on the downtown square.

"Can I help you, sir?"

"I'd like a room, please." Jake tried not to stare, but the pouty, lipstick-red mouth and fiery green eyes seemed familiar.

She slid a form and a ballpoint pen across the counter with fingers whose nails were painted the same red as her lips.

Jake filled in the information and pulled a credit card from his billfold. When he glanced up, she stared at him, eyes wide, lips parted.

"Something wrong?" he asked.

"Jake Reynolds, is it really you?"

He grinned. "I hope so. Want to check my ID?"

She smiled back at him. "You don't recognize me, do you?"

Something about her expression sparked a memory. "Kay?"

"Yes."

He reached out to shake her hand, but she shook her head and came around the corner of the desk. "I want a hug."

Jake returned the hug. "It's good to see you. You look great."

"So do you." She returned to her place behind the counter where she filed his registration card away.

"Tell me you haven't lived here all this time," Jake said. "What happened to the girl who had big dreams about being a flight attendant?"

Kay shrugged and leaned against the counter. "I gave up that dream a long time ago. Went to business school instead."

Jake glanced around the lobby. The retro style furniture reminded him of his childhood. He could have chosen one of the more modern hotels out on the freeway, but he preferred a more laid-back style, and this old building filled the bill.

"Do you own this place?"

Kay shook her head. "No. Jonathan Woods still owns it."

Jake nodded. "He's still around, huh?"

"Yes. He's eighty-five-years-old, so I help out. Besides, it gives him a chance to go fishing." Kay turned to a row of keys on the wall and selected one. "Come on, I'll show you to your room."

Jake grinned. "Now that's service for you. I bet they wouldn't treat me this good at the big motel out on the freeway."

Kay chuckled. "We like to make our guests feel at home, like they're special."

Jake followed her down the hall until she stopped in front of a door. She opened it and stepped aside to let him enter. "How's this one?"

The spacious room glistened in the late evening sunlight pouring through the window. Although the rose-patterned wallpaper was faded in places, the antique furniture and hardwood floors sparkled. The large four-poster bed in the center of the room looked inviting after his long drive.

"Works for me. How long has this motel been in operation? I know it's been here ever since I was a kid."

"Mr. Woods says it was built in 1910." Kay handed him the key. "I don't think much has changed since then. He says he's going to keep it open as long as he's alive. We don't do much business, except for the salesmen who have been coming through and staying with us for years. They keep coming back out of loyalty to him. We don't have air conditioning, so it can get pretty uncomfortable at times, but the ceiling fan works, and we have extra oscillating fans if you need one. How long will you be staying?"

Jake set his suitcase on the floor and tossed the key on the dresser. "I'll only be here long enough to decide what to do about Aunt Nora's house."

"Oh, yes, the one on Orchard Street. I wondered what would happen to it when you didn't come home."

"I should've come back sooner, from the look of things."

Silence hung between them for a few seconds before Kay spoke. "What *did* bring you back after all these years?"

"I got a letter from a land developer named Sheridan, threatening seizure of the property. Sounds like he has a lot of influence."

Kay frowned. "More than most people like. Between him and the town council, things are getting hot around here, and it's not Texas heat either." She paused and looked at Jake for a moment. "How do you feel about Dale after all this time? He's on the council, so you'll run into him if you're here for long."

He shrugged. "It's history." He walked over to the window and pretended to look out at the town square.

"No hard feelings?"

Jake swallowed the bitter taste in his mouth. "I just hope I don't have to see him."

Silence filled the room, and Jake turned. She was looking at him in utter surprise.

"You're still carrying a grudge after all these years?"

"Call it what you want, I don't want to run into him."

"It was a long time ago, Jake. They're divorced."

"Yeah." He didn't want to rehash the past with Kay. He changed the subject. "Is there a good place to eat around here? I'm starving."

"Garrett's Café is the only place in town other than the Dairy Queen and the truck stop out on the highway. But I guarantee you won't be disappointed in the food at Garrett's. I'm planning to go there after work myself. You're welcome to join me."

He noticed she had no ring on her finger. "Sure, if you don't mind my company."

Kay glanced at her watch. "Mr. Woods should be back soon. I'll knock when I'm ready to leave."

After Kay closed the door, Jake walked over to the window for a closer look at his old hometown. Like a lot of small Texas towns, the courthouse sat in the center of a square surrounded by other businesses. Archer Springs's old red brick courthouse looked the same, but some of the other shops on the square were abandoned, their windows boarded.

A sign still hung over Brown's Drugstore. Jake glanced at one corner of the big picture window, at a small paper poster from his childhood. He couldn't read it but he knew what it said. *Come inside. It's air conditioned.* A kid could walk in on a hot day and order a glass of ice water. Roy Brown didn't care if you didn't have money. He knew you'd come back some other day with fifty cents in your pocket and order a cold, creamy root beer float. Everyone knew whose kid you were, and they treated you right.

In those days, he had never thought about living anywhere else. He had planned to spend his life here, raising a family and growing old with Marilyn, but life didn't always follow a man's agenda.

Jake glanced at the names of other businesses on the square. Most of them were new tenants in the same old buildings. One of them caught his attention—Sheridan Holdings Company. The guy who'd forced his return to this place. *Well, Mr. Sheridan, you can expect a visit from me tomorrow morning.*

Jake turned from the window and reached for his suitcase, to freshen up a bit before his dinner date. He smiled to himself. There'd been a few women in his life, but it had been a while. After years of playing the field, and almost marrying a couple of them, he'd grown tired of the game. None of them had been able to erase Marilyn's memory. It wouldn't have been fair to the women or to himself to marry if he was still in love with someone else, even if he kept telling himself he wasn't.

Tonight would be nothing more than a good meal with an old friend. And he needed that. He didn't have a lot of close friends, and sometimes the loneliness became unbearable. Part of the fault fell on him. He found it hard to allow anyone to get too close.

Jake sighed and stuck his hand in one of the side pockets of the suitcase for his toothbrush. As he pulled it out, a faded piece of pink ribbon fluttered to the floor. He bent to retrieve it. Yesterday, as he was packing, he'd opened the dresser drawer and pulled it from its hiding place and stuffed it inside the suitcase. He'd never been able to throw the ribbon away. Maybe he'd be able to dispose of it here, in the town where he'd obtained it.

He squeezed his hand around the satin remnant from the past. The memory of the night he'd pulled it from Marilyn's hair came rushing back. An old familiar ache raced through his chest. He had tried discarding the ribbon several times through the years, but always found himself digging through the wastebasket to rescue the shiny fabric before he discarded it for good. Jake stuffed the ribbon back into the side pocket and headed for the bathroom where he discovered a claw foot tub. No shower.

He stripped down and settled into the tub of hot water. He was tempted to relax for a while, but instead he bathed quickly, toweled off, and dressed in a clean shirt and a fresh pair of jeans. He was brushing the dust from his boots when Kay knocked on the door.

"Are you ready, Jake?"

IIe opened the door and stepped out into the hallway. She smiled with approval. "You clean up pretty good."

In the lobby, an older man was nursing a glass of iced tea. Jake recognized him as the owner, Jonathan Woods. As a kid, Jake had thought of Mr. Woods as a large man with a fierce countenance who chased him and his friends away from the front of the motel when they tried to shoot marbles on the sidewalk. Now the older man was stooped and didn't even reach Jake's shoulder—his once black hair had turned snow white.

A smile crept across Mr. Woods's face as recognition dawned. He extended his hand. "Jake, my boy, welcome home. It's been a long time."

Home? The word sounded foreign to him. He didn't think of Archer Springs as home. Jake shook the frail, bony hand, which seemed to get lost inside his own.

"Thank you, Mr. Woods. How are you? Kay tells me you've been doing some fishing."

The old man leaned his head back and laughed. "Did she tell you I don't ever catch anything? I spend most of my time asleep on the bank while the fish eat my bait."

Kay patted his arm. "Don't be so hard on yourself. The fish have to eat too." She reached for her purse on the counter. "We're going to Garrett's. Can we bring you anything?"

"No, thanks. I'm going to eat a bowl of corn flakes and turn in early." Mr. Woods slipped his arm around Kay's shoulder, then looked at Jake and pointed one of his bent, arthritic fingers at him. "You take care of this little lady. She's one of a kind."

Jake nodded. "Yes, sir, I will."

Mr. Woods winked at him. "A pretty young thing like this shouldn't be sitting home every night by herself. She'd make someone a fine wife."

Jake could tell the old man's affection for Kay ran deep. Living in the same small town all your life could forge that kind of relationship. He didn't have that kind of bond with anyone. Not anymore.

Kay blushed. "We'd better get going. We don't want to miss the blue plate special." She took Jake's arm and steered him out the front door and away from Mr. Woods.

"Is he telling the truth?" Jake asked as they rode to the cafe. "Do you sit at home by yourself every night?"

Kay shrugged. "I guess I do, but there's not a horde of admirers beating a path to my door either. Archer Springs is a little short on available men."

"You never married?"

Kay shook her head. "Guess I never met the right guy ... well, once upon a time, but as you said, it's history."

Jake glanced at her again, wondering if Dale had been her right guy, but he didn't ask. Everyone had a right to their privacy. He pulled into the last empty space in the café parking lot and killed the engine.

A simple, handwritten sign inside the door said, "*Please seat yourself.*" Every pair of eyes in the room stared at them as he and Kay made their way to an empty table. "I feel like I'm on display," he whispered as he pulled out a chair for her.

Kay grinned. "All visitors to Archer Springs get the same treatment."

A waitress with a blonde ponytail appeared, jotted down their order and left, returning with two glasses of iced tea.

Jake looked around the crowded room. Red leather booths lined the four walls. Local artwork hung over each one, a small white price tag noticeable in the corner of each frame. Tables—placed so close together you could help yourself to your neighbor's plate—filled the center of the restaurant. "Must be a popular place."

"You'll know why when you sink your teeth into Mattie Garrett's food." Kay added a packet of artificial sweetener to her iced tea and tasted it. "Tell me about yourself. Are you married? Have a family?"

Jake shook his head and forced himself to smile. "I'm afraid our situations are much the same."

Kay sipped her tea and then set the glass down. "I know it's been a long time ago, and I hate to bring up the past, but I want to make things right." She hesitated and cleared her throat. "I'm sorry I was the one to tell you about Marilyn and Dale. I regretted sending the note once I'd had time to think about what it would do to you."

Jake shrugged. "I guess I should thank you. I had to find out sometime ... somehow. If you hadn't sent the note telling me they'd married, I would have looked like the biggest fool in Texas when I came back. I guess I was anyway."

"Be honest with me, Jake. Did my note keep you away all this time?"

Jake took a deep breath before answering. He didn't want to hurt her, but he wouldn't lie about it. "Yes, to be honest, it did."

Kay's eyes brimmed with unshed tears. "I'm so sorry, Jake."

He reached across the table and touched her arm. "Forget it. No hard feelings."

Kay tried to smile, but it was a weak one. "Did they ever try to contact you?"

Jake nodded. "I got a letter from Marilyn a couple of weeks after yours came, but I burned it." A vivid memory flashed through his mind. He'd been raking leaves when the mail carrier delivered the envelope. When he saw the name *Marilyn Summers* in the top left-hand corner, he hadn't even bothered to open it. He had thrown it onto the pile of leaves, struck a match and then held it to the paper until it curled into ashes. What could she have to say to him now that she belonged to someone else?

"Have you ever wondered what she wrote in the letter?"

Jake sighed and reached for his glass. "Yeah, but in a way, I guess I was afraid to know." He shrugged. "It didn't make a whole lot of difference. They were already married."

The waitress appeared with their food. Jake, grateful for a diversion, dug with passion into the chicken-fried steak, mashed potatoes, and black-eyed peas. It had been hours since he'd eaten. "You were right about this food," he said between mouthfuls.

While they ate and exchanged small talk, Jake listened to the buzz of conversation around him. Everyone talked across the room about their crops, their grandchildren, or their new tractor. A camaraderie existed here you didn't find in a big city. These people shared a history—the same history he could have had if he hadn't left. A trace of sadness swept over him.

Darkness had moved in by the time they drove back to the motel, but the heat from the day still hung in the air. Streetlamps gave a soft glow to the town square. It felt peaceful. No sirens screamed, no cars raced down the street, a much different environment from the city. Jake parked in front of the motel, and they stepped out of the truck.

"Can you talk for a while?" He grinned. "Or is it past your bedtime?"

Kay smiled and sat down on a bench in front of the motel. She patted the seat beside her. "What are your plans for your Aunt Nora's house?"

Jake joined her. "I intend to go see Sheridan first thing in the morning to find out what his intentions are."

"Jake, be careful."

He couldn't read her face in the dim light of the motel vacancy sign. "What do you mean?"

"Sheridan is a sly one. He's got more tricks up his sleeve than there are mosquitoes in Texas."

"I've dealt with people like him before. Atlanta is full of Sheridans."

From somewhere on the square voices carried through the night. Jake couldn't understand what they were saying, but he spotted a group of people who appeared as dark forms standing on the sidewalk. "What's going on over there?"

Kay's voice dropped a notch.

"It's Sheridan's office." She shook her head. "I wouldn't be surprised if they're conspiring to take over the town."

Jake laughed in spite of the concern he heard in her voice. "I heard someone say something similar earlier today. How can a group of men take over an entire town? This is America, remember? You vote them out when the time comes." He stopped laughing when she didn't agree with him. He sensed her uneasiness.

"Word around town is there have been threats to people who bucked them. Walt Miller refused to sell them his old house at the edge of town, even though he hasn't lived there in years. Last week, it burned to the ground. The newspaper called it faulty wiring, but I'm sure it was Sheridan's doing."

Jake nodded. "Carl Malone told me people were losing their homes. Wasn't there an investigation?"

"A phony one." Kay slapped at a mosquito on her arm. "The fire chief said faulty wiring, and no one argued with him. He's one of Sheridan's buddies." She sat silent for a moment. When she spoke again, her voice was laced with sadness. "So is Dale. He and Sheridan seem to get along well." She crossed her arms over her stomach. "I wish he hadn't gotten mixed up with him."

Jake's skin crawled at the mention of Dale's name. He watched as the men across the street called their goodbyes to one another, climbed into their vehicles, and drove away into the darkness. He wondered which one was Dale, but he didn't ask.

After several minutes spent discussing the changes in the town over the last two decades, Kay stood. "I need to go so you can get some rest. You had a long drive today."

Jake walked with her to her car. "Thanks for the dinner invitation."

She nodded. "Will I see you again before you leave?"

"I'll be here for a day or two. I'm sure we'll run into each other again."

After Kay left, Jake sat in the sultry darkness, reluctant to return to his room. The more modern motels had air-conditioning like his apartment in Atlanta, where he kept the thermostat at a costly but cool seventy-two degrees. Perhaps he should have stayed at one of those places out on the interstate.

He leaned back against the building and marveled again at the quietness. The only sound came from crickets and tree frogs. Jake looked skyward. He had forgotten how brilliant the stars could be on a clear summer night. His grandfather had taught him to identify the constellations when he was a boy. Orion, the Big Dipper, and the Seven Sisters sparkled above him. Living in the city had erased such pleasures as star gazing.

The sound of an engine broke the night's calm. An older model white Volkswagen approached. It slowed to a stop at the motel and sat there, engine idling. When Jake noted the driver peering at him, he moved toward it. The car accelerated and sped away. Jake watched it vanish from sight and then went into the motel lobby.

Mr. Woods sat behind the reception desk reading. He looked up as Jake came in.

"Did you and Kay have a nice time?"

Jake nodded. "She's good company." He frowned. "I thought you were turning in early."

Mr. Woods shrugged.

"Reading makes me fall asleep, but not tonight." He folded his newspaper and tossed it on the counter. "I don't know how I would make it if Kay didn't help me." He reached below the counter and brought out an oscillating fan. "It's going to be a hot one tonight, Jake. Better take this with you so you can sleep. The motel is empty except for you and a couple of others so if you need another one, feel free to ask."

Jake accepted the fan and thanked the older man. Inside his room, he opened the window and undressed in the dark. He lay down on top of the sheets. The room felt like a sauna. It would be nice to get back home. He closed his eyes and drifted into sleep.

Sometime later, he awoke with a start. His body felt damp from the heat, and he sat up. Other than the whir of the fan, silence filled the room. He climbed out of bed and stepped to the window. An orange glow danced in the sky, and the faint odor of smoke floated through the open screen. He remembered what Kay had told him about the Miller place burning down.

Jake grabbed his jeans and pulled them on. He snatched his shirt from the bedpost and jerked open the door.

Sheridan, for your sake, it better not be Aunt Nora's house.

Jake ran toward the burning house, his bare feet pounding against the pavement. A siren sounded in the distance. The orange glow he'd noticed from his motel window grew bigger and brighter by the minute. He rounded the corner onto Orchard and slowed, heaving a sigh of relief. It wasn't Aunt Nora's.

As he moved closer, he heard the pop and crackle of burning wood. The temperature of the summer evening blended with the intense heat of the fire made the atmosphere suffocating.

Firemen sent a spray of water into the blaze, useless against the fiery tongues devouring the old timber-framed house which stood across the street from Aunt Nora's.

All along the street, people stood in their yards staring at the destruction. A few feet away, a man and a woman talked in hushed tones, oblivious to Jake's presence.

"You s'pose this one was set too?" the woman asked.

"I'm sure of it," the man said. "They tried to get the owner to sell and he refused."

"It's only a matter of time before there are others. The old Reynolds house across the street is vacant, too. It'll be next."

A wave of apprehension rolled over Jake. He wanted to shout they were wrong. He wasn't going to let some greedy hotshot real estate developer from a backwoods town push him around. But he kept quiet. It wouldn't be wise for a stranger to be vocal about the situation. He would have to use his head plus a lot of common sense if he wanted to save Aunt Nora's house from the same fate.

Jake watched until the flames died. Nothing remained except a pile of smoking, glowing rubble. People drifted back to their homes. Jake made his way to the motel alone. At the corner of Orchard and Main, he noticed the same white Volkswagen he'd seen earlier idling across the street.

The driver, who sported a ponytail, leaned over the steering wheel, absorbed in the fire scene. He didn't even notice Jake walk by.

Marilyn Summers tossed the remote control on the sofa and ran her hands through her shoulder-length brown hair. One would think she'd be used to being alone by now. It had been a mistake to leave Archer Springs and move to a town where she knew no one.

She added the sofa pillow behind her and sank into its cushiony softness. Thanks to Dale, the generous divorce settlement had enabled her to buy a new condo. She had decorated it in the soft pastels she loved, creating what she thought would be a relaxing haven, but nothing could ease the loneliness surrounding her day after day.

The house felt like a tomb. Marilyn tuned the radio to her favorite AM station. Maybe some classical music would make her feel better. Dale had never cared for classical music, saying, "It's a bunch of sophisticated noise. No one in Archer Springs listens to it. What's wrong with country, or the old fifties music we used to listen to?" Truth be told, she didn't love it too much herself.

Marilyn slipped into the comfort of the sofa, closing her eyes and letting the music flow over her.

The truth was songs from the fifties—hers and Jake's—were too painful to hear. When she listened to them, she would close her eyes, and his face, his arms, his lips would all be there, all so real.

On the morning he'd left with the harvesters, she woke early, dressed and was at the town square before they left. When Jake saw her, he smiled. They walked a short distance away from the others, and he pulled her close.

"Marilyn, remember this. You're the most important person, the most important thing ever in my life. Please wait for me."

To her shock, tears formed in Jake's eyes. She had never seen him cry. She reached up and touched the wetness on his cheek. He hugged her close and kissed the top of her head as the truck convoy pulled up before the courthouse.

Jake gathered his belongings and walked toward the other men. They boarded the truck, and he waved to her from an open window as they drove away.

She never saw Jake again. It had been twenty-five years. *Twenty-five years.*

Mozart had done nothing to blot out her memories tonight.

Kay climbed into bed and reached for the novel on her bedside table. She read a few lines, but her mind kept drifting back to earlier in the day. Jake Reynolds was the last person on earth she expected to see walk into the motel. Those blue eyes were as vibrant and full of fire as ever, along with evidence of someone who had experienced a lot of anguish, more than he should have.

A pang of guilt coursed through her. She'd been the one to tell him about Marilyn and Dale. But someone had to tell him, and he didn't seem to hold any ill feeling toward her for doing so. At the time, she had felt he had a right to know before he came back to Archer Springs, expecting to marry Marilyn.

She sighed. The four of them had such good times when they were younger. She and Marilyn had been best friends since elementary school and the two boys had been like brothers joined at the hip. But they weren't kids anymore, and life had changed for all of them.

Kay closed the book and laid it on the bedside table. Time had been good to Jake. He could still turn heads. She had noticed the female patrons in Garrett's staring in his direction, and it wasn't because he was a stranger in town.

He could turn my head. If my heart didn't belong to someone else.

CHAPTER 2

MONDAY, JUNE 7, 1982

Jake gave James Sheridan enough time to unlock his office the next morning before he walked across the street to meet with him. The receptionist greeted him as he entered the office.

"Good morning," she said, her smile rivaling the bright yellow dress she wore. "Do you have an appointment with Mr. Sheridan?"

Jake shook his head. "No. My name's Jake Reynolds. I'm here about a letter Mr. Sheridan wrote me."

The receptionist held up one finger. "One moment, please. She disappeared into a back office.

Jake paced around the waiting area. Expensive-looking oversized armchairs and a sofa filled the room. A large glass-topped table held a magnificent vase, and a fancy coffee service rested on a marble-topped counter against one wall. Fresh flowers sat on the receptionist's desk. Rather lavish for a small-town businessman.

The receptionist reappeared. "Mr. Sheridan will see you now."

A man about Jake's age stood as Jake entered the office. A large mahogany desk dominated the center of the room, surrounded by matching bookshelves on three walls. Jake's boots nearly disappeared into the thick burgundy carpet as he walked across the floor.

James Sheridan smiled and reached across the desk to shake Jake's hand.

"Mr. Reynolds, good to meet you."

Jake couldn't help noticing the expensive silk suit and designer tie Sheridan wore and the Rolex gleaming on his wrist when they shook hands. They didn't quite fit the image of the rest of Archer Springs, with its working farmers and ranchers. His fingernails were too clean.

"Have a seat, Mr. Reynolds. Can I get you a cup of coffee?" Without waiting for Jake to answer, he turned to the receptionist. "Diane, bring us two coffees." He glanced at Jake. "Cream, sugar?"

"Black." Jake sat in the chair Sheridan indicated and sank into cushioned luxury.

"Now, Mr. Reynolds, what's on your mind so early in the morning?"

Jake pulled the envelope from his shirt pocket and pointed it at Sheridan. "I'm here about the letter you sent me."

A smile curled the corners of Sheridan's lips. "Oh yes. The property on Orchard Street. Well, you seem like a reasonable man. I'm sure we can come to an agreement on the selling price of the house."

Jake cleared his throat. "My aunt wanted the property to remain in the family. Since I'm the only living family member, the decision is mine. I'm not interested in selling."

Sheridan tapped a stack of papers with a Mont Blanc pen and scowled. For a fleeting moment, Jake saw anger flash in his eyes, but Sheridan forced a smile and maintained control.

"Impossible, Mr. Reynolds. We're condemning all the old houses in town. You may as well sell it to the city. I can have Diane write you a check while we have our coffee and get acquainted. We're paying homeowners five thousand dollars for their property at this time."

Jake leaned forward in his chair. "Five thousand dollars? That's highway robbery."

The flash of anger appeared again, but still Sheridan kept his voice even. He studied Jake for a moment, his eyebrows knit in a faint frown.

"Robbery is a strong term for our transactions. Your property is an eyesore in our charming little town. We're in a renovation program here in Archer Springs, and we're on a tight budget and a tighter schedule. If you want to unload your property, you'd best do it while we've got the funds, and you're offered the chance to walk away with some money in your pocket."

Jake gritted his teeth. "Who's doing this condemning and making these offers?"

"The city fathers and myself."

Jake doubted the city fathers had much to do with it. The scent of greed swirled around the man sitting across from him. "And what gives you or them the right to condemn someone's house?"

Sheridan closed his eyes. When he opened them, the coldness they reflected chilled the room.

"Archer Springs is a small community. We don't have all the organizations larger cities do. We work with the people we have to make this a better place for everyone." A thin smile appeared on his lips. "Shall I have Diane write you a check?"

Jake glared at Sheridan. "I don't think you understand. My property isn't for sale."

Diane came in with the coffee and conversation came to a halt. She served her boss, then handed Jake a cup. He watched Sheridan add cream and sugar to his coffee. The property owners in Archer Springs might not be getting rich, but he had a feeling the scoundrel with the Rolex was benefiting at the expense of the townspeople.

Jake stood and set his coffee cup on the expensive desk.

"Mr. Sheridan, thanks for your offer, but I'll pass." Jake made it to the door before Sheridan spoke.

"Reynolds, you're a determined man. I like that. We may be able to do business yet, but my offer won't last forever."

Jake didn't respond. He walked out of the office without looking back. When he reached the motel, Mr. Woods met him at the front door.

"Kay called for you earlier." He nodded toward the desk. "You can use my phone."

Jake dialed the number and took deep breaths to bring his pulse back to normal. She picked up on the first ring. "Had breakfast yet?"

Jake sighed. "No, but I could use some after the meeting I just walked out of."

"Uh-oh. That doesn't sound good. Come on over. We'll talk while we eat."

The big white frame house on Magnolia Street looked as Jake remembered it. Fresh paint, mowed yard, and marigolds planted on both sides of the walk. Even as a teenager, Jake had admired the Carter home. It took a lot of sweat, water, and persistence to keep a yard healthy during a sweltering Texas summer. Some were more successful than others.

The front door stood open. Jake rang the bell anyway.

Kay appeared in a pink sundress and sandals. "Come in. Everything's ready."

As he entered and brushed past her, a pleasant scent greeted him, reminding him of ripe strawberries. He took a deep breath, enjoying the fragrance, and followed her to the kitchen.

The breakfast table invited him to pull out a chair. A vase of fresh flowers sat in the center of a blue and yellow tablecloth, with matching place mats and napkins. A plate of fresh grapefruit and orange slices along with silver and crystal for two completed the picture.

Jake let out a low whistle. "You didn't have to go to all this trouble for me. I'm a bachelor, remember?"

"It's no trouble." She set a plate of bacon, eggs, toast, and hash browns in front of him, then filled one for herself.

Jake laughed. "Do you have this kind of breakfast every day?"

"Hey, this is a special occasion. It's not too often I get a chance to entertain. Besides, it's a reunion of sorts. We're celebrating your return." She poured coffee for them and spread a napkin across her lap. She looked at Jake. "Would you like to say grace?"

No one had asked him to pray in twenty-five years. His mother had insisted on it when he was a kid, and Aunt Nora had always prayed at mealtime, but none of his associates in Atlanta prayed before eating.

"I wouldn't know where to begin."

Kay smiled. "It's all right. I'll do it."

The simple prayer left Jake feeling uncomfortable. Lots of people said grace when they ate. Not him, of course. He had given up praying years ago, after his last night with Marilyn. What had transpired that night wasn't something he was proud of.

He reached up and pulled the ribbon from Marilyn's ponytail. The smell of the lavender scent she always wore floated around them. His grandfather's words faded in and out of his consciousness like a radio station interrupted by a stronger frequency. "Jake, don't ever let your emotions override common sense. You'll be sorry if you do."

Jake shook off the memory and glanced at Kay. She was staring at him, a puzzled expression on her face.

"You okay?"

He nodded and poked at the eggs with his fork. "I guess my visit with Sheridan rattled me a little."

Kay poured orange juice and handed him a glass. "Mr. Woods told me you left early, so I assumed you went to his office. How did your meeting go?"

"After the fire last night—"

Kay set her glass down hard enough to slosh juice over the rim. "What fire? I didn't hear a siren."

"The house across the street from mine burned down last night." Jake added salsa to his eggs and took a bite. "This is delicious."

"The Thomas place?" She shook her head. "It's been vacant for quite a while, too. What did Sheridan say about your property?"

Jake spread blueberry jam on his toast before answering. "He offered me five thousand dollars for it."

Kay shook her head again. "Five thousand dollars isn't much compared to the sentimental value of the place, is it?"

"I know the house isn't worth much, considering the condition it's in, but I refused his offer." Jake thought her face paled a little.

She set her fork down, her eyes full of concern. "What was his reaction?"

Jake shrugged. "He said his offer wouldn't last forever." He took another bite of eggs. "This salsa is really good."

"Thanks. It's made fresh by a local woman. You should stop by her place before you leave town." A mischievous smile crossed her face. "Bet they don't have anything this good in Atlanta." She added cream to her coffee and took her time tasting it before she spoke again.

"Watch Sheridan. He's charming, but shifty."

Jake shook his head. "I didn't see any charm oozing from him. And shifty is really too nice a word."

Kay helped herself to a slice of grapefruit and passed the plate. "Let's change the subject. Tell me what you've been doing all these years."

"Not much to tell. After I got your letter, I knew I couldn't come back here. I ended up in Atlanta, Georgia, where I went to junior college. Then, I started working for a plastics firm and finally, made general manager. Nothing glamorous, but it's a living. What about you?"

"I went to business school, and then came back here to help Dad in the insurance office. After he died, I closed the office and went to work for Mr. Woods." She sipped her coffee before continuing. "Most of our crowd left and never came back. Dale and I are the exceptions."

Jake finished his breakfast and pushed the plate to one side. "What does Dale do besides serve on the town council?"

"He has a real estate office in town. After he and Marilyn married, he got his real estate license, and his dad set him up in business. He built a big house on the outskirts of town." Kay eyed him over her coffee cup. "Are you sure you want to talk about this?"

He shrugged. "You're the one who said it was a long time ago."

"I know, but I get the feeling it seems like yesterday for you."

Jake changed the subject. "How did Sheridan get into the picture?"

"He was a friend of Judge Wilson. Two years ago, he blew into town and opened an office. Judge Wilson introduced him around as a college buddy. The next year, Wilson was diagnosed with cancer and died three months later. Sheridan has been on a rampage ever since, attempting to control the entire town."

"Sounds as if he's done it. What's in it for him? I take it not everyone likes him. Carl Malone seemed a little bitter about it."

"Most of the older people don't trust Sheridan. He promises the younger ones all kinds of good things are going to happen to Archer Springs. So far, I haven't seen anything good happen to anyone but him." She pointed to his cup. "Want a refill?"

"No, thanks. I've had plenty." He scooted his chair back and stood. "Thanks for breakfast. I've enjoyed our visit, but I need to get going."

"What are you planning to do?"

"I need to see what it'll take to get the house ready to sell."

A puzzled look crossed her face. "But you said ..."

He held up both hands. "I know. I told Sheridan it wasn't for sale and it isn't, not to him. Aunt Nora wanted it to remain in the family, but there's no way I can live in Atlanta and maintain a house here. The least I can do is make it livable again for someone else."

"Sheridan isn't going to like you crossing him."

"Maybe not, but I made a promise to my aunt, and I intend to keep it."

"There are a few things you don't know."

"Such as?"

"There's been a horrible drought the past three years. Most of the farmers have suffered big losses that affected the entire town." Kay sighed. "Even the bank threatened to close. Sheridan offered to take on some of the mortgages the bank was holding. He saved the bank, and people were able to keep their homes."

"So he's not only blackmailing them, but he also holds the mortgages on their houses." Jake shook his head. "What a scoundrel. Either you do what he wants, or you lose your home—either by fire or repossession. Is your house involved in this?"

She shook her head. "No. Daddy paid off our mortgage before he died." She placed her hand on Jake's arm. "What I've told you is confidential. Don't let on to anyone you know about this. It'll put the whole town on the defensive. Their homes are at stake."

"How could the town folks allow themselves to be taken in by Sheridan?" He stared at her for a moment. "And how can you and the others keep your mouths shut and let him do it?"

"Because if we speak up, too many people get hurt. We keep hoping someday there will be an end to all of it."

"An end may well be in sight, but it may not be the kind you're hoping for."

Jake left Kay's house and headed toward his own property. As he pulled up in front, he groaned at the amount of work needed to make the house livable.

He walked through with a pen and pad, scribbling a list of supplies he needed for the renovation. Paint, glass for the windows, new doors, flooring. He wiped sweat from his forehead and added 'air conditioner' to the list. He also needed to hire a plumber and an electrician. He would buy lumber and repair the floor and porch himself. He glanced at the roof and added it to the list. It would take a nice chunk of his savings to restore this relic.

Oh, well. It's not like I have a family to support, or kids to put through college.

As Jake walked through the house, he realized his original plan to stay for a couple of days wouldn't be long enough. He'd need to use some of his vacation time to get this place in shape. He'd call his boss when he got back to the motel.

He stopped in the hallway to jot more notes and glanced toward the ceiling. A short piece of frayed rope hung from a hook. He stretched and pulled it, and the attic door came down with a bang along with an army of bugs, dust, and cobwebs. He waited for the air to clear, then climbed into the attic.

Nothing appeared to have been disturbed for years. Cardboard boxes, stacked two and three high, stretched across one end of the space. Discarded cobwebby furniture stood like familiar skeletons from the past. Jake poked around in boxes full of canning jars, old clothes, and a set of outdated encyclopedias until he spotted a wooden box behind the stacks. *Aunt Nora's treasure chest.* She used to hide her important stuff in the box—things nobody else would want, she always said—and no one was allowed to open the chest, not even Uncle George. She'd threatened everyone with their life if they touched it.

Jake pulled the chest from its hiding place and brushed off the layers of dust.

"Sorry, Aunt Nora. I'm going to snoop." He used his pocketknife on the rusty lock, and it squeaked open. He raised the lid and let it fall back against the floor.

Some old 45s rested on top of the contents. He picked up a handful and read the titles. *Sixteen Candles. The Great Pretender. All I Have To Do Is Dream. Only You.* The titles sounded like his old record collection. But how had Aunt Nora ended up with his records? He had given them to Marilyn before he left. Unless Marilyn gave them to his aunt when she and Dale married.

Jake stacked the records on the floor and turned back to the chest. His senior year portrait smiled up at him. He picked it up and turned it over. *To Marilyn, with all my love, Jake.* He stared at the words for a moment, and a hot sweetness washed over him until he shrugged it off and tossed the picture on top of the record stack. When he turned back to the chest, he saw it. A half-heart on a gold chain. The half he had given to Marilyn.

For a mere second the world spun around him like an old forty-five record. Jake slammed the lid on the box, and the serenading images vanished into the past.

CHAPTER 3

The next morning, Jake returned to the house with cleaning supplies. As he pondered which room to start on first, Kay appeared.

"This place smells terrible." She covered her mouth and nose with her hand. She walked around the room, sidestepping garbage. "It's a complete wreck."

He nodded. "It's going to take a lot of work to whip this place into shape." He opened a box of heavy-duty garbage bags and tore one off the roll.

Kay reached for the bags. "Where do you want me to start?"

Jake shook his head. "This isn't your problem." He looked around the room. "No telling what we might find in all this filth. I'll handle it."

"But I want to help. This job is too big for one person." She winked at him. "Besides, it gives me a good excuse to spend time with you."

He grinned and handed her a pair of gloves. "Okay, if you insist, but you don't need an excuse to spend time with me." He wondered what she meant by the statement as he watched her head toward the kitchen, bag in hand. The blue-striped blouse and denim shorts looked nice on her well-tanned body. He looked away. He had too much to do to be admiring a pretty woman.

A voice drifted in from the porch. "Hello. Anybody home?"

"In here."

A young man with red hair and a generous sprinkling of freckles stepped inside the front door. "I'm Harold from Archer Springs Water Supply."

Jake nodded and held out his hand. "You're just in time, Harold. We're getting ready to clean this place."

Harold grinned, causing the freckles on his face to appear even larger. "You'll have water as soon as I check everything out." He wrinkled his nose. "That's some smell you've got in here."

It took all morning to clear the debris, sweep dirt from the rooms, and dismantle the cobwebs. Then they began cleaning walls and floors, scrubbing them with heavy-duty brooms and a combination of bleach and soap. Paint rubbed off in places, leaving the bare wall exposed. Jake had finished the last wall in one of the bedrooms when Kay wandered in.

"I'm getting hungry. How about you?"

Jake wiped his forehead with the back of his hand. "I agree. We've worked right through lunch. My stomach's growling, and I'm exhausted. Let's call it a day."

She appeared tired too. A black smudge almost covered her nose, and her hair hung limp and damp around her face. The place had been filthy. He shouldn't have let her help.

"Can I take you to dinner in exchange for your labor, or would you rather go home and rest?"

She wiped her face with a paper towel. "I'm starving. Give me time to go home and clean off the grime."

Two hours later, Jake and Kay finished their meal of roast beef, new potatoes, and green beans at Garrett's, then sat back to enjoy coffee and blackberry cobbler.

Kay sighed and closed her eyes. "I don't know about you, but I found some new muscles today."

Before he could answer, a tall broad-shouldered man in faded jeans and a denim shirt approached their table. He held out his hand.

"Hi, I'm Paul Brown. Harold from the water company told me you're fixing up the old Reynolds place."

Jake nodded. "Yes." He shook Paul's hand. "Jake Reynolds."

Paul glanced over his shoulder as if looking for someone, then he turned back to Jake.

"Are you planning to live there?"

Jake shook his head. "Nope. I'm hoping to sell it."

The noise level in the room dropped and everything went silent. Every ear in the café seemed tuned to their conversation. Jake looked around. Several pairs of eyes stared at him. He didn't realize he had spoken loud enough for the whole room to hear him. Maybe they had been watching and listening ever since he and Kay had arrived.

Paul rubbed the mustache gracing his upper lip and frowned. "You may have a hard time selling."

"How come?" Jake knew how Kay and Mr. Malone felt about the situation, but he wanted to hear other opinions. He waited, but Paul offered no explanation and neither did anyone else.

"Nice to meet you, Jake." Paul nodded at Kay, then returned to his table. The other diners went back to their own conversations and coffee cups. A few stood and made their way to the door, glancing at Jake as they passed.

Jake leaned across the table and spoke in an undertone. "Did I say something wrong?"

Kay shook her head. "No. It's what's happening in town. They're all on edge." She reached over and placed her hand over his. "You'll be leaving in a few days to go back home, but these people have to live here. I know it's hard to believe, but Sheridan has a lot of influence here. He and the town council are making decisions that affect everyone in Archer Springs."

Jake nodded but didn't voice what he was feeling. They finished their coffee and cobbler and walked outside.

Paul Brown stopped them as Jake opened the truck door for Kay.

"Sorry if I was a little abrupt in there. I'm sure Kay has filled you in on the trouble we have around town. These folks don't have anything against you—they just have families and businesses to think about." Paul started to walk away, then looked back at Jake. He glanced around as he had in the restaurant, then lowered his voice. "Don't underestimate Sheridan. He's dangerous."

During the drive home, Kay stayed quiet. Jake caught her looking at him when they stopped at the signal light in town.

"Something wrong?"

She smiled. "You know, you haven't changed much."

Jake chuckled. "How do you know? All you can see is the outside. You don't know anything about the man on the inside. He's been through some major changes."

"The man on the outside looks the same to me." She grinned. "Except for that hint of distinguished gray on your temples. As for the inside, well, that's not my department."

When they reached her house, he walked her to the door.

Kay turned to face him. "Would you like to come in for a while?"

Jake shook his head.

"Thanks, but I want to get an early start in the morning. I think I'll turn in and get some sleep." He looked down at her. He brushed a strand of dark hair away from her forehead, and she smiled. A warm feeling stirred him inside, but he pushed it away. He knew his priorities and they didn't involve the heart beyond protecting his family's property and seeing it sold to someone honest, someone who truly wanted it. He let his hand drop.

"Thanks for everything. You've been a big help."

Jake arrived at the motel to find Mr. Woods watching television in the lobby. He stopped at the counter to watch the news with the older man. The world hadn't changed much in the last forty-eight hours. Jake's aching muscles convinced him it was time to call it a night, but something the newscaster said stopped him cold.

"An explosion at Masters Manufacturing, the leading producer of plastic products in the South, awakened residents in Atlanta, Georgia early this morning. Several smaller explosions followed, destroying the main plant."

Pictures of a smoldering building flashed onto the screen. The reporter continued. "An investigation is under way as to the cause of the blast. Masters is the main competition for Texas Plastics Incorporated located in Dallas. A spokesman for Texas Plastics said this could mean an increased workload for them in the coming weeks and months."

Shock swept over Jake. "You've gotta be kidding. This can't be happening."

Mr. Woods looked up from the screen. "Something wrong?"

Jake pointed at the television screen. "That's where I work." He shook his head. "I can't believe what I'm seeing."

Mr. Woods shook his head. "I'm sure sorry, Jake. This must be quite a blow."

"Guess I better call and see what's going on. Mind if I use your phone?"

"Go right ahead."

Jake dialed Art's private number but got the answering machine. He decided to try Charlotte Watson, Art's private secretary. She picked up on the first ring.

"Charlotte, this is Jake. I saw the newscast."

"Oh, Jake, it's awful." Charlotte's voice cracked. "It looks like a war zone, and they don't have any clue why it happened. We're all out of a job, unless Art rebuilds the business."

He gripped the phone tighter. "Is there a chance he won't rebuild?"

"When I asked him, he was rather evasive, but he did say the insurance should take care of the building."

"How's he taking it?"

"You know Art. Nothing's important except his money and the business. He's been moaning and wringing his hands for hours. And he's been looking for you."

"Will you give him this number for me? He can reach me here." Jake gave Charlotte the number of the motel and placed the receiver back on the phone a few moments later.

In his room, Jake undressed and lay down, his mind reeling with questions. *If I go home and see about my job, what happens to Aunt Nora's house? That's easy. Sheridan will tear it down.*

The siren woke him an hour later along with the smell of smoke filtering through the open window. *Not again.* He pulled on his clothes and slung open the door. In the hallway, he ran into Mr. Woods in his bathrobe.

"There's another fire somewhere," Jake said. He hurried to the front door and jerked it open. A familiar, red-orange glow lit the sky over Aunt Nora's house.

Thick black smoke billowed toward him and burned his lungs. He slowed his steps, but kept walking toward the fire, breathing a sigh of relief when he saw it wasn't his house. Flames rose from the house two doors down. He stood across the street and watched the firemen fight the blaze. Like the other old house, the inferno roared out of control. Jake heard someone crying and looked around.

A woman, barefoot and dressed in a thin gown, sobbed.

"What are we going to do? We've lost everything." A man standing next to her, wearing only a pair of jeans, didn't answer. He pulled her into his arms and held her while she cried. The light from the fire shone on his face. Hopelessness in the shape of a tear trickled down his cheek.

Jake felt sick to his stomach. Until now, Sheridan had been burning empty houses. This one had been occupied.

Anger surged through him. How far would this man go to get what he wanted? A chill crept up his spine. He glanced at the grieving couple again, almost afraid to consider it. He turned and walked back to the motel.

Mr. Woods waited on the porch. "Was it your place?"

Jake shook his head. "No, it was two doors down. And it was occupied."

Mr. Woods made a clucking sound with his tongue.

"This is not good. People burning other folks' property. I'd bet my best Sunday suit this is Sheridan's doing, but how are you going to prove it? He's hired somebody else to do his dirty work for him." The old man turned and went into the motel.

Jake sat down on the bench outside the door, repulsed by what he had witnessed the past two nights. Every day, there was more evidence of the corruption in Archer Springs. An expression he had often heard his grandfather repeat crossed his mind. *Dirty lawyers, slippery carpenters, and backslid preachers. You can't trust 'em.* Grandpa might have been right about the carpenters and the lawyers. Jake didn't know much about preachers.

He heard a car engine and glanced up. The same white Volkswagen from the night before puttered along the street. Jake stood. He had questions he wanted answered.

The driver gunned the engine and sped away.

CHAPTER 4

WEDNESDAY, JUNE 9TH

The next morning, a knock on the door awakened Jake. He opened his eyes and blinked in the bright morning sunlight streaming through his window.

"Phone call for you," Mr. Woods said.

"Can you take a message?"

"I think you'd better come. He's insisting on speaking to you."

Atlanta. Art, about the business.

Jake pulled on his jeans and padded down the hallway barefoot, buttoning his shirt as he walked. He took a deep breath before answering.

"This is Jake."

"If you know what's good for you, you'll go back where you came from." The voice sounded muffled, as though a cloth had been placed over the receiver.

"Who is this?"

"It doesn't matter. Take my advice. Get out of town."

Last night's anger resurfaced. "Look, I don't know who you are, but—"

The phone went dead. He replaced the receiver and went back to his room. Maybe he should accept the offer from Sheridan. Take the five thousand dollars and go home.

But what about my promise to Aunt Nora?

It didn't matter now. Aunt Nora would never know if he didn't keep his promise to her. How much was a promise worth anyway? An image of Marilyn floated through his mind. It sure hadn't meant anything to her.

On the other hand, I don't have a job to go home to. Just because the rest of the world doesn't keep their word is no reason I have to follow suit.

He dressed and drove to Garrett's Café for breakfast, the air still reeking of smoke. The place was empty except for two white-whiskered men in overalls. As he walked past their table, he could hear them talking in low tones about last night's fire. Jake chose a table as far away as possible and ordered eggs over easy and grilled ham from the waitress.

"Where is everyone today?" he asked, as she poured his coffee.

"They've come and gone. You're late." She pulled out a chair. "May I?"

Jake shrugged. "Sure, why not." One of the hazards of small-town life. No privacy.

She poured coffee for herself.

"You don't remember me, do you?" She cocked her head to one side and smiled.

He sipped his coffee and studied the face before him. Purple eyeshadow and bright red lipstick did nothing for her appearance. The blonde hair pulled back in a ponytail gave her a girlish look, but the tiny lines around her mouth and eyes betrayed her age. Another middle-aged woman trying to look younger. He glanced at her name badge. *Mae.* He shook his head.

"No, I'm afraid I don't."

"I'll give you a hint. You were Dale's best friend in high school. You dated Marilyn and he dated Kay."

He laid down his fork and leaned back, the muscles in his neck growing tight. "How do you know that?"

"When you came in with Kay the other night, I thought you looked familiar." She rested her elbows on the table. "Don't you remember a smart-aleck cousin who used to visit Dale every summer?"

Against his better judgment, Jake let his mind wander back to the past. The ponytail evaporated into pigtails as he remembered. "Clara Mae."

She wrinkled her nose. "I never did like the Clara part, but Mother made me go by Clara Mae. When I graduated from school and left home, I dropped Clara. Now it's just Mae." She refilled his cup. "Have you seen Dale since you've been back?"

He cleared his throat. "No, I haven't." *And don't want to.*

"You and Marilyn were engaged at one time."

The last bite of egg lodged in his throat. He swallowed and took a sip of coffee. "At one time."

She leaned forward, lowering her voice.

"What they did to you wasn't right, even if Dale is my cousin." She winked at him. "I think that marriage was a mistake from the beginning. I never could understand why they got married. You could tell they weren't in love. More like friends if you ask me."

Jake pushed his chair back and stood. He pulled a five from his billfold and dropped it on the table.

"Excuse me. I need to be going." He strode toward the door.

"Sorry if I upset you," she called after him. "Didn't mean any harm."

Jake nodded and kept walking. "No harm done."

He drove to the house, forcing the conversation out of his mind. He gathered his tools and began replacing broken windowpanes. The plumber arrived a few minutes later. Jake showed him the bathroom problem and went back to work.

By mid-afternoon, the windows shone with new panes, the plumber had replaced the bathroom fixtures, and everything worked. He scrubbed every inch of the bathroom and then painted the kitchen. Later that evening, he inspected the results of his labor. The house looked different, smelled better. Maybe he should stay here while he was in town. It would save some money, a necessity now that he'd lost his job. And it might save the house. He put his tools away and headed for the motel.

Kay sat behind the desk typing on an ancient Underwood typewriter. Jake grinned and tapped the machine with his finger.

"I didn't know any of these still existed."

She smiled. "Mr. Woods isn't interested in modern technology." She pulled the sheet of paper from the carriage. "How's the renovation going?"

He rubbed his eyes. "My eyes are full of sawdust and paint shavings, but I got a lot accomplished. If I could scrape together some furniture, I think I might move in."

She looked surprised. "I thought you were going to list it for sale."

"I am, but meanwhile, who knows what Sheridan will do? It might keep him from burning it to the ground." He shrugged. "I've slept on the floor before. It won't kill me."

"Mr. Woods has some furniture in storage. I'll ask him about it when he gets back."

"Great. Now, if you'll excuse me, I'll get this paint and dirt scrubbed off." He started down the hallway, then stopped. "How about dinner?"

She flashed him a sparkling smile. "I'd love to, but aren't you getting a little tired of taking me to Garrett's every night?"

Jake shook his head. "Never. I'd be a fool to pass up the chance."

An hour later, they arrived at Garrett's, found a corner table and ordered. Jake noticed they didn't seem to attract as much attention as the first time they'd come. A couple of men nodded at him when he and Kay passed their table. A woman called out to Kay, and she waved back. While they waited for their food, he told her about the telephone call he'd received that morning.

Kay's eyes widened.

"You've got to be careful. Do you think Sheridan had something to do with it?"

Jake shrugged. "Maybe, but I'm not giving up. This guy's getting under my skin. I've been here for three days, and already I've seen two houses burn, been offered to have my own house practically stolen for five thousand dollars, and been ordered out of town by an anonymous caller." He jabbed the tabletop with his finger. "I'm not going to run from this fight."

She laughed. "Now you sound like the old Jake. Remember how you used to defend Dale when anyone said something bad about him? You'd tear into them like a bear. And he'd do the same for you."

He nodded. "I'd forgotten about that." Over the years, the betrayal and bitterness had clouded anything good from those days. All his memories of Archer Springs had been angry and pain-filled.

"I don't know how you could forget all the scuffles you and Dale got into defending each other. Kay chuckled and shook her head. "Those were good times."

The waitress brought their order, and they ate in silence for a few moments. Then Kay laid down her fork.

"I almost forgot. I asked Mr. Woods about the furniture. He said take whatever you need."

"Thanks. I'll check on getting electricity tomorrow, and then look in his storage room." When they finished their meal, he paid the check, and they headed for his truck.

"How do you feel about a late evening drive?" Jake asked as they pulled away from the café.

Kay leaned her head back against the seat. "Sounds good."

He didn't have a particular destination in mind, but a few minutes later he turned toward Pearce's Lookout. It wasn't really a hill, just a rise with a short drop off above the town. Teenagers often brought their dates here because it was the most romantic spot around. As he pulled into the area, nostalgia swept over him, and he shivered. His last visit here had been with Marilyn.

He turned to Kay, but she already had the door open.

"I haven't been here in years." She climbed out of the car. "The four of us used to come here all the time, remember?"

As if I could forget.

He joined her and reached for her hand. "Want to see the lights of Archer Springs?"

A soft laugh escaped her lips. "Of course. But I'm the one who should be showing you. You're the guest in town."

They walked to the edge of the hill and gazed at the sleepy town below. Twilight had fallen, leaving the sky a dark purple. A half-moon appeared overhead, and the evening's first stars looked like tiny diamonds winking at them. Lights glowed in the windows of homes where families were sitting down to their evening meal. Archer Springs looked peaceful. No one would ever guess a corrupt contractor schemed down there behind closed doors, wreaking havoc among the townspeople.

A slight breeze stirred, a welcome reprieve from the heat of the day. Somewhere in the distance a whippoorwill sounded a mournful cry. Jake slipped his arm around Kay's shoulders, and she moved closer. He could feel the warmth of her body and smell her perfume. He closed his eyes. A voice in the back of his mind sounded a warning bell.

You're on dangerous ground.

He opened his eyes and looked at the scene below again. This time he saw the single flashing red light in the center of town. It seemed to be sending him a message.

Stop! Stop now before this goes any farther.

She turned to face him. "You're too quiet. What are you thinking about?"

Jake looked down at her. The moonlight gave her face a luminous glow. Her lips looked inviting.

"You." Jake pulled her closer. He closed his eyes, and an image of Marilyn flashed before him. He lowered his lips to hers.

She pulled away from him, and Jake opened his eyes, shocked to see Kay's face instead of Marilyn's. For a few seconds, he had allowed memories of the past to take over. His reaction must have been evident because she looked away from him. He dropped his arms and swore under his breath, shame flooding through him.

"I'm sorry, that shouldn't have happened."

"It's okay."

"No, it's not okay. I'm a heel for—"

"Forget it. It didn't mean anything." Kay reached over and touched his arm. "We were caught up in the moment, in this romantic setting."

Jake looked at the town below. The lights didn't seem quite as bright now. The magic of a few moments before had vanished. "Guess this wasn't such a good idea."

"It was a great idea." She caught his hand in hers. "Let's go back to the motel and see if Mr. Woods has some ice cream in the freezer."

Later, alone in the sweltering motel room, Jake berated himself for his behavior. Kay didn't deserve to be hurt or used. *She's a beautiful woman, but she isn't the one I want.*

He climbed out of bed and walked to the window, hoping for a cool breeze. Thank goodness no orange glow lit the sky tonight. No sirens pierced the stillness. Sheridan wasn't destroying the peace tonight.

He pulled on a pair of jeans and slipped out to the front porch, barefoot and shirtless. He sat on the bench and stretched out his legs, grateful to find a place a few degrees cooler. The quietness felt like a soothing hand against his anguished mind. He could get used to this feeling of semi-peace. This, and the right woman, could change his life.

CHAPTER 5

Thursday, June 10th

The next morning, Jake rubbed sleep from his eyes and stumbled across the floor to answer the door. Mr. Woods smiled at him. The older man looked far too energetic for this time of day.

"How about joining me for breakfast? Nothing fancy. Hot biscuits with butter and plum jam and a cup of coffee is all I can offer you. Or a bowl of cereal, if you like corn flakes."

"Be right there." Jake dressed and combed his hair, then walked across the hall.

Inside Mr. Woods's quarters, the older man pulled a pan of biscuits from the oven and set them on the table.

"That homemade plum jam came from the church bazaar last year at First Presbyterian. It won first place, so I bought a few jars. This year's event is in September. If you hang around, you can buy some to take home with you."

Jake buttered a biscuit, spread jam on it, and took a bite.

"I don't plan on being here that long. It's good, though. Reminds me of Aunt Nora's." He took another bite and washed it down with coffee. "I appreciate your offer of furniture."

"No need to thank me. Somebody ought to get some use out of it. It's been in storage ever since my wife passed." He shook his head. "Ten years, and I still miss her. You don't get over the kind of love we had. Comes once in a lifetime."

Jake's heart wrenched inside his chest. *I know all about that kind of love.*

They ate in silence for a moment before the old man spoke again.

"I noticed you and Kay are spending quite a bit of time together." He paused for a few seconds, then went on. "That's good, maybe. Depends on your intentions. She needs a good man, but she doesn't need to be wined, dined, and then abandoned." He stood and walked over to the counter for more coffee.

One thing about the old man. He didn't mince words.

Mr. Woods poured second cups for them and sat back down.

"You know, son, when two people care about each other, it's a wonderful thing, but a one-sided relationship can hurt innocent people."

Jake stopped spreading jam on his second biscuit and glanced at Mr. Woods. "Is there something you want to say to me?"

The old man cleared his throat and looked at Jake. "Don't run off and leave her like you did Marilyn Baker all those years ago."

Jake's knife clattered against the table, leaving purple jam on the tablecloth. He stared at the old man who kept right on eating as if he delivered that kind of bombshell every day. Jake dropped the biscuit he was holding onto the plate.

"Is that what you think? Is that what everyone in Archer Springs believes? That I abandoned Marilyn?"

Mr. Woods shrugged. "Appears to most people that you did."

Jake gritted his teeth. "I didn't abandon her. She married someone else behind my back. Someone I *thought* was a friend. They betrayed me. What they did is unforgivable."

"Maybe." Mr. Woods set his coffee cup down. "But anything can be forgiven if you're willing to put it behind you."

Jake jumped up, turning over his coffee cup. The black liquid splattered across the table and dripped off the side. "Sorry," he mumbled. He opened the door and hurried from the room before Mr. Woods could say anything more.

He strode out the front door of the motel and drove to the house, struggling to keep his thoughts rational and his emotions under control. His hands trembled on the steering wheel. It wasn't until he stepped onto the porch that his angry mental battle came to an abrupt halt.

The front door stood open.

When he stepped into the living room, a wave of rage swept over him. Large red streaks covered his freshly painted white walls. An empty spray can lay in one corner.

Sheridan.

He swore and hit the doorjamb with his fist. He checked out the other rooms. The culprit had been at work there too. He pounded on the desecrated wall.

"I'll get you for this!" he yelled to the empty house. His body shook from the anger pulsing through him. He leaned over the kitchen sink and splashed cold water on his face to calm down.

No matter what Sheridan does, I've got to keep my head if I want to survive this thing. At least he didn't burn it. Not yet.

Jake heard a sound like a smothered scream and stepped into the living room. Kay stood just inside the front door, her eyes wide, staring at the desecrated walls.

"Oh, no. What happened?"

"I'll give you two guesses." He rubbed his sore knuckles, thinking the doorjamb made a poor substitute for Sheridan's face.

She walked around the room, inspecting each wall.

"Did you call the sheriff?"

"No. Do you think it would do any good?"

"It's worth a try. You can't keep painting the house every day." She reached out and touched one of the red slashes of paint, then jerked her hand back as if from a hot iron. Or blood.

"It might be a good idea if I went ahead and moved in. Maybe that would discourage any more vandalism."

"Don't be too sure," she said. "Sheridan doesn't stop until he gets what he wants."

He grabbed a paint roller and a bucket of paint. He had stopped trembling, but anger still simmered beneath the surface. "Well, there's no use standing around talking about it. It has to be redone."

Kay glanced around the room again. "Do you have an extra roller?"

It took three coats to cover the red paint, but by mid-afternoon, the walls glowed pristine white again.

They cleaned the rollers and put everything away, then drove to the motel to get Jake's things. When they arrived, Mr. Woods greeted them from the desk where he sat reading the paper.

"How's the house coming along?"

Kay slipped her hand around Jake's arm. "It's looking great, but Jake had some trouble last night. Somebody sprayed red paint all over the walls. We had to repaint them."

Mr. Woods clicked his tongue. "That's a shame. I guess we all know who pulled that stunt."

Jake exhaled. Every bone in his body ached.

"Mr. Woods, I'm going to check out of the motel and move into the house."

Alarm flickered in the old man's eyes. "You think that's wise?"

Jake shrugged and held his hands up in defeat. "After last night's vandalism, I think it's best." He reached for his wallet. "What's the balance on my bill?"

Mr. Woods folded his paper and laid it to one side. "You don't owe me anything. I enjoyed the company. It's good to have you here in Archer Springs again. You'll need that furniture, though."

"That's not necessary." Jake hesitated to accept the old man's generosity with the scene at breakfast still fresh in his mind. This day had been a spinning wheel of emotions and he felt drained of strength, but most of all he was ashamed of the way he had stormed out of Mr. Woods's kitchen, angry and rude.

"Nonsense," the old man said. "Somebody may as well get some use out of it." He tottered off down the hall. Jake followed, shame nipping at his heels.

Mr. Woods unlocked the storeroom door and pushed it open. "Paul Brown's got a flatbed trailer he might let you use. He's a good man, always willing to help people. I'll call him while you see what you need."

The room looked like an antique store. Everywhere he looked, furniture from decades past hovered in the shadows. Not only were there pieces from the early 1900s, but several retro pieces caught Jake's eye. He selected a red and gray plaid armchair that looked almost new. He spotted a matching sofa and went over to inspect it. An old record player sat on one end. He remembered the 45s in the attic and made a mental note to ask Mr. Woods about borrowing the player later. A butcher block table with two matching chairs sat in one corner. He would need it in the kitchen, along with the hotplate sitting nearby. A mattress and springs rested against one wall. Jake checked the mattress for holes and decided it would do.

Mr. Woods stuck his head in the door. "Paul's on his way."

Twenty minutes later, Paul pulled in front of the motel with his trailer, and they loaded the furniture and headed for Jake's house.

"I hope you make a go of it here," Paul said, as they set the last piece of furniture in place.

Jake reached out to grasp the younger man's hand. "You don't know how much I appreciate your help and your friendship."

Paul shook his head. "Time was, everybody would be your friend and help you. Things have changed around here." He walked out to the porch, then looked back at Jake. "If you run into trouble, holler."

"Thanks."

After Paul left, Jake and Kay arranged the furniture, and Kay made the bed with some linens from the motel.

"Thanks for helping me get set up here, but you'd better get going," he told her when they were done. "I don't have electricity yet, and I don't want you here when it's dark in case trouble comes calling."

They stepped out onto the porch, into the twilight. A gorgeous sunset greeted them. Jake pointed at the evening sky, brilliant with streaks of red and gold.

"Nothing like a Texas sunset, is there?"

She smiled. "I wouldn't know. I've never been too many places. Never seen a sunset anywhere else."

Jake stuffed his hands in his pockets and stared at the vivid colors. "Trust me. Nothing like it."

As they walked to her car, Jake glanced down the street. The white Volkswagen sat idling at the corner.

"Do you know who drives that vehicle?"

She nodded.

"Yes, it belongs to Monty Summers, Dale and Marilyn's son." She frowned "Wonder what he's doing in this part of town?" She squinted at the vehicle. "But that doesn't look like Monty driving it."

CHAPTER 6

For a moment, Jake didn't know where he was when he opened his eyes on his first morning in the house. Then it all came rushing back. He had moved into Aunt Nora's house yesterday. He climbed out of bed and dressed, then headed for his truck. He had nothing to eat in the house and no way to cook anything, at least not yet. He needed and wanted electricity in the house to show it was occupied. Maybe whoever was responsible for the red paint on his walls would think twice before doing it again.

He drove to the power company office to inquire how much longer it would be.

The middle-aged matron behind the desk peered over her reading glasses at Jake. "We have other service calls ahead of you. I told you that the last time you were here. You have to wait your turn." She pushed a stray lock of graying hair away from her forehead with manicured red nails. "You drugstore cowboys are all alike." She pulled off her glasses and looked down her nose at him. "Just because you wear expensive boots and come from the city doesn't mean you can cut in line."

Jake wanted to wipe the smirk off her face, but he knew he wouldn't. Not only wouldn't but couldn't. If his parents had taught him anything, it was respect for women. Never mind that they didn't always respect you. He had learned that many years ago, thanks to Marilyn. He turned away from her taunting eyes. As he did, he noticed a sign on a closed door to his right. *Supervisor.* He walked to the door, tapped once, and entered. Behind him he could hear Ms. Smirk shouting for him to stop.

Jake closed the door. A man looked up from his paperwork, a startled look on his face. "Can I help you?

Jake smiled and extended his hand. "I'm Jake Reynolds."

The door flew open, and Ms. Smirk rushed in.

"I'm sorry, Mr. Dobbs. I told him he couldn't come in here." The lock of hair had fallen down across her forehead, and the smirk had disappeared.

The man looked at her, then back at Jake. "It's okay. I'll handle it."

Ms. Smirk squared her shoulders and pushed her hair into place. "I told him he'd have to wait his turn."

"It's quite all right, Elizabeth," Dobbs said. "I can handle this matter."

"Well, if you're sure ..." She backed out of the room, but not before giving Jake a withering glance.

He smiled and tipped an imaginary hat in her direction.

"Now, what seems to be the problem?" Dobbs asked, after the door closed behind the receptionist.

Jake explained about the vandalism and fires in his neighborhood. The man's face turned pale as he listened.

"... so as you can see, sir, I need to have some lights at my house."

Dobbs shook his head. "Don't worry, Mr. Reynolds. I'll send someone out this morning. You'll get your power." He stood and walked to the door with Jake. "Sir, I don't know who you are, but I'm afraid you picked a bad time to move to Archer Springs." Dobbs glanced around the room as if he expected someone to be hiding there. "Frankly, if I were you, I'd pack up and leave here as soon as possible."

Jake didn't ask for an explanation to his statement. Nor did he try to explain his reason for being in Archer Springs. "Thanks for your help."

As he passed by Ms. Smirk's desk, he hesitated. Maybe he could practice being a peacemaker on her. He leaned toward her, placing both hands palms down on her desk. "It takes a lot fewer muscles to smile than to frown. You might want to try it sometime."

Something bordering on hatred blazed in her eyes. "Get your hands off my desk."

He knew he'd pushed things far enough.

"Good day to you, ma'am."

She tilted her nose in the air and turned her back to him. *So much for peacemaking.*

Jake chuckled as he walked out of the office. At least he could still find some humor in the situation, albeit short lived.

He made a quick stop at the local general store for a coffeemaker, toaster, and some groceries. When he passed a display of insulated coolers, he grabbed one. He would need a place to store perishables until he found a refrigerator.

The power company truck pulled up in front of the house as he unlocked the front door. Mr. Dobbs was on the ball.

"That was quick," Jake said, as the paunchy, middle-aged man approached the porch.

The man shrugged and gestured vaguely to his left.

"I was working on the next street over. Mr. Dobbs called and said to get over here right away. I figured it must be an emergency, so here I am."

"Thanks, I appreciate it."

Kay arrived soon after, minus her usual smile, looking as though she hadn't slept too much the night before.

He frowned. "Are you okay?"

She shook her head.

"I have some bad news. Dale had a heart attack last night."

Hearing Dale Summers's name didn't sit well with him, but he didn't say anything. Kay gave him an incredulous look. "You don't care?"

"People change. I haven't seen him in twenty-five years. I don't even know him now. I'm sorry about the heart attack, but Dale isn't a part of my life anymore."

When she spoke, her voice came out in a whisper.

"Can't you leave the past where it belongs and forgive him?"

"We don't owe each other anything."

"Even if he wants to see you?"

Jake gave her a sour look. "Why would he want to see me? To ease his guilty conscience? It's a little late for that, don't you think?"

Kay sighed and shook her head. "Give him a chance, Jake. Like you said, people change. You weren't the only one who got hurt when they married."

"What are you talking about?"

She played with the silver bracelet on her arm, moving it up and down as though trying to find a comfortable place for it. "Maybe it would help if you heard my side of the story."

Jake frowned. "What do you mean, your side of the story?"

She looked at him, her forehead creased, as if in deep thought.

"You remember how the four of us double-dated every weekend? Well, what happened that summer after graduation affected all of us."

He waited.

"I used to think Dale and I would end up together some day. He didn't seem interested in anyone else, and we were a couple for a long time, even if it wasn't too romantic." She shrugged. "I knew it wasn't like you and Marilyn. We didn't have that kind of relationship, but we shared an awful lot in those days. The four of us were inseparable until you left. My feelings ran pretty deep."

Surprise rippled over Jake. "You mean, you ...?"

Kay nodded, tears shining in her eyes.

"I was in love with Dale."

He shook his head, shocked to hear her confession. "I'm sorry. I had no idea."

"No one did, except Marilyn. Not even Dale himself. I didn't want to push him into a relationship he wasn't ready for. After you left for Kansas with those harvesters, we only went out together a few times, and then everything came to a halt. You remember how close Marilyn and I were—best friends since elementary school. One day, she quit calling and wouldn't return my calls. It wasn't long before I found out why."

She blinked. "I went to work one morning, and the phone started ringing off the wall. Everyone in town wanted to know if it was true Dale and Marilyn had eloped. They were asking the wrong person, because I didn't know anything about it."

Jake shook his head. "Guess we both got the shaft, huh?"

Kay reached across the table and placed her hand over his.

"It almost destroyed me, trying to live with all that anger and resentment. It would have, too, if I hadn't forgiven them. It wasn't easy, but I did it. God gave me strength to accept the past and put it behind me."

"I'm not so sure it would bring me peace to give Dale something he doesn't deserve. It won't change what happened. It won't bring back those lost years."

"You have to try. What if Dale doesn't make it? Are you going to spend the rest of your life wallowing in bitterness?" She shook her head, sadness brimming in her eyes. "It'll destroy you."

He frowned.

"Too much time has passed. If I hadn't come back, I wouldn't have known he was dying, and it wouldn't have changed anything. I would still be living with what they did. Besides, if anyone should beg for forgiveness, it should be him, not me."

Without opening his eyes, Dale Summers knew he was in the hospital. The oxygen tube in his nose sent a continuous stream of air into his nostrils. He moved his left hand and felt the soreness from the IV. The faint voices of nurses reached his ears. He ran his tongue over his dry lips, almost tasting the antiseptic aura of the place. He searched his memory for the reason he had been brought in.

His conversation with Sheridan came rushing back with so much force his chest heaved, bringing with it the recollection of the intense pain and pressure of the heart attack. He'd been almost home when it hit him. As soon as the familiar pain radiated across his chest, he'd reached inside his pocket for his nitroglycerin pills. They weren't there.

He'd stopped the truck in the driveway, not bothering to open the garage, and stumbled inside the house. He kept some nitro in his bedside table, if he could just make it up the stairs. The next jolt of pain almost sent him to his knees. He'd made it onto the first step and sat down, struggling to breathe.

This is it. It's happening and I can't do anything about it. It's over for me. Then the front door opened, and Monty walked in.

"Son, get me my nitro pills. They're on my bedside table." He couldn't remember anything after that.

Dale opened his eyes. Almond-colored walls and blinking monitors greeted him. He turned on his side and felt a breezy sensation on his back. He looked down at the hospital gown in disgust. *Might as well not be wearing anything as to wear this rag.* It left him feeling naked and exposed to whoever walked through the door. He tugged the sheet higher on his body.

He closed his eyes and felt himself drifting. *Must be all the medication.* Before he slipped into oblivion again, he remembered something else. Jake was back. He smiled to himself.

It's about time, old buddy. I've been waiting for you for years.

After Kay left, Jake walked out on the porch and sat on the top step. Weariness tugged at every muscle in his body. He knew Kay was right about putting the past behind him, but he was the victim in this situation, not the villain. Why should he be the one to grovel?

A Bible verse Aunt Nora used to quote to him all the time surfaced in his mind. She had said it to him so often he could remember her reciting the words like it was yesterday.

But I say unto you, Love your enemies, bless them that curse you, do good to them that hate you, and pray for them which despitefully use you, and persecute you.

If he remembered right, it was found in the book of Matthew, but the chapter and verse escaped him. She used to remind him of it every time he got into a scrape at school. But this went beyond a mere scrape.

He stared out across the sunbaked yard. It was at the end of a blistering day much like this one that he'd received Kay's note about the marriage. He would never forget that day as long as he lived ...

The foreman waved an envelope in his direction. "Hey, Reynolds, mail for you."

Jake frowned at the letter. It wasn't Marilyn's handwriting. He tore open the envelope and unfolded the single sheet of paper. It was a letter from Kay informing him of Dale and Marilyn's marriage. He stared at the letter, paralyzed by the words. He didn't realize tears were running down his face until the foreman asked him if it was bad news.

"You need to go into town and make a phone call?" the foreman asked.

They found a gas station whose attendant allowed Jake to use the phone and pay in cash afterwards. Jake called Marilyn's house. Her mother answered. He felt as though he might pass out when she confirmed Marilyn and Dale had married. He ran from the gas station, running from the reality of the news, until the foreman's truck pulled alongside him and honked.

The next day, Jake claimed his pay and left the harvesting job. His reason for being there had vanished. The sympathetic foreman drove him to the main highway and wished him good luck. Jake caught a ride with the first truck that came along and rode to the driver's destination— all the way to Atlanta, Georgia.

He closed his eyes against the painful memory, but it didn't work. Nothing could exorcise this ghost. He heard the gate squeak and opened his eyes.

Mr. Malone shuffled up the sidewalk and stopped. He wiped his forehead with a blue bandanna. "Morning, Jake."

"Good morning, Mr. Malone."

Carl Malone looked around at the house, nodding his head. "Old place is lookin' up."

"Yeah, but there's still plenty to do yet." Jake rubbed his eyes and stretched his sore muscles.

"Takes time, my boy, takes time," the old man said, easing down to sit on the steps. "Anything worth doing takes time."

"I shouldn't have let it get in this condition."

Mr. Malone turned toward Jake. His sharp look seemed to penetrate right into Jake's face. "Why did you?"

Jake glanced away. One thing about Malone—he spoke his mind, like Mr. Woods.

"Too many bad memories."

"Son, you can't keep running from the past. The way to heal a wound is to treat it." He squinted at Jake in the morning sun. "Have you heard about Summers's heart attack?"

"Yes, sir. Kay told me."

Malone hooked his fingers together and twiddled his thumbs. "A dying man needs peace before he goes."

"You think he's going to die?"

Malone frowned. "I don't know, but one thing I do know. You're not the only one who's suffered all these years. I imagine Summers has spent some sleepless nights, too."

Jake gritted his teeth. "He deserved them. I didn't."

Malone shook his head. "If we all got what we deserved, we'd be in deep trouble."

"Maybe so, but this is one time I'm not guilty." Jake stood. "Would you like some ice water or a soda?"

"No, thanks. You go ahead."

Jake went inside and grabbed a soft drink from the ice chest which served as his refrigerator for the time being. He popped the top and took a long drink from the can before returning to the porch.

Mr. Malone continued the conversation as though Jake had never left.

"We've all made mistakes, but it's not good for a man to carry bitterness around in his gut. It eats away at you like cancer, and sooner or later it'll destroy you. If I were you, I'd go see Summers, get this thing straight so he can be at peace and you can too. You know what the Good Book says. 'Blessed are the peacemakers.'"

"Yeah, I know. The book of Matthew. But I'm not a peacemaker. I've been at war in one way or another ever since I left here."

Malone rubbed his whiskery chin. "Maybe it's time you laid down your weapons and quit fighting."

73

Jake swallowed the last of his soda and set the empty can on the step. He looked out across the yard, uncomfortable under the older man's probing stare.

"If I quit fighting, they win." He sighed. "I'm not a good loser."

Malone stood and started down the sidewalk. At the gate, he turned and looked at Jake.

"Peace comes to them that make peace. No matter who wins or loses."

He walked out of the yard without looking back.

Jake sat on the steps for several minutes, lost in thought. Mr. Malone had disappeared, but his words rang in Jake's ears like church bells on Sunday morning. He stood and picked up the empty soft drink can and wondered how badly he wanted peace.

Late that afternoon, as he finished painting the porch, Kay pulled up in front of the house. She came up the sidewalk, her face edged in sadness. Jake wiped the sweat from his forehead.

"More bad news?"

She nodded. "I've come from visiting Dale in ICU. Monty shared his visiting time with me."

"How is he?"

"About the same." She opened her purse. "He asked me to give you this." She handed Jake a folded piece of paper.

He stared at the note. He didn't want anything Dale had to offer, but he didn't want to hurt Kay, either. He unfolded the sheet and read the words spidering across the paper.

We need to talk. I need to explain. Dale

CHAPTER 7

SATURDAY, JUNE 12TH

The next morning, Jake made coffee, poured himself a cup and then sauntered into the living room just before the window imploded and blew razored missiles of broken glass into the air in front of him. He flung his hot coffee away, dropped to the floor, and wrapped his arms around his head and face. After a few seconds, he raised up enough to look around.

Flames roared from the center of the old armchair he'd borrowed from Mr. Woods. He grabbed a pillow from the couch and beat at the fire. Sparks floated in the air as the noise of a car engine floated in through the broken window.

Hurrying to the window, Jake spotted a white Volkswagen as it turned the corner and disappeared. He swore. Monty Summers must have thrown something at the house. That sorry scumbag must be working with Sheridan. *Like father, like son.* He made sure the chair fire was out, cleaned up the spilled coffee, and then headed for his truck. A few minutes later, he stopped in front of the sheriff's office.

A young deputy looked up as Jake entered the office. "Can I help you?"

Jake forced himself to stay calm. "I'd like to file a complaint. Someone tried to set my house on fire a few minutes ago."

The young officer paled when Jake said the word *fire*. He stared at Jake as though he were a ghost. Jake drummed the countertop with his fingers.

"Aren't you supposed to ask me some questions and take down information? I want to file an official complaint against the person who started the fire."

The deputy's eyebrows went up in a quizzical look. "You know who did it?"

Jake sighed in frustration. "I have a pretty good idea."

"You can't file a complaint on a pretty good idea. I need a name." The young officer tapped the pad in front of him for emphasis.

Jake took a deep breath before answering.

"Look, someone threw a bottle—maybe a Molotov cocktail—through my window. It caught a chair on fire. If I hadn't been there, the whole place would have burned. I saw a white Volkswagen drive away from my house right after it happened." He shook his head and gripped the counter with both hands. His attempts at composure were wearing thin. "I know there's at least one in town, and I know who owns it. There can't be that many white Volkswagens in Archer Springs."

The deputy held up his hand. "Okay, okay. I'll run it through the system and see what I can find out. Meanwhile, sir, try to remain calm."

"Easy for you to say." Jake turned on his heel and headed for the door. He left the sheriff's office, doubting anything would be done. This whole town consisted of two groups: Sheridan's cronies and his victims. You either agreed with him, or you were his target.

Reaching home, Jake surveyed the damage. The chair was ruined, and pieces of broken glass lay beneath the window. He had replaced that window once already. He should send Sheridan a bill. Sunlight streaming into the room reflected off the glass in a prism of vibrant colors around the window. Pretty, but there was nothing pretty about what Sheridan was doing.

As he swept up the debris, Jake spotted the crumpled note from Dale lying under the edge of the sofa. He opened the paper and read it again. After all this time, Dale wanted to explain. Why explain? The damage had already been done. And Marilyn shared the guilt with Dale, maybe even more so. Anger washed over him. He tossed the note into the dustpan and threw it out with the rest of the garbage.

He made a list of what he needed to repair the window and headed for the hardware store. After making his purchases, he drove to the motel. Finding the lobby empty, he knocked on Mr. Woods's door. The old man greeted him, coffee cup in hand.

"Come in, Jake." He held up his cup. "Want some?"

"Sounds good." Jake pulled out a chair and sat down.

Mr. Woods poured coffee and set a cup in front of him.

"I had a fire at the house this morning," Jake said.

"Jumping Jehoshaphat. Is your house gone?"

"No, but your chair is."

Mr. Woods laughed. "Fiddlesticks. Is that all? That chair was almost as old as I am. What happened?"

"Someone threw a bottle through my window that landed in the chair and set it on fire."

"Sheridan's doing?"

"I'm sure of it. I haven't told anyone else, but every time there's a fire, I've seen a white Volkswagen at the scene. This morning, I saw the same car pulling away from my house. Kay said it belongs to Monty Summers."

Mr. Woods shook his head. "That can mean only one thing. Young Summers is in cahoots with Sheridan. Sheridan should be strung up by the heels for involving young people in his corruption."

"Does he also have the law under his thumb?"

"Wouldn't surprise me at all. Why? Did you file a complaint?"

"I tried. As soon as I said the word *fire*, that deputy backed off like he'd seen a rattlesnake." He wiped a brown drip off the side of his cup. "I don't expect anything to come of it."

Mr. Woods sipped his coffee. "He either suspects Sheridan, or he works for him, one of the two."

Jake drained his cup. He knew the time had come to bring up their last breakfast conversation.

"Mr. Woods, I want to apologize for my actions the other day."

The old man looked at him over the top of his coffee cup but didn't say anything. Jake cleared his throat and swallowed hard. He wasn't used to apologizing to people.

"There's no excuse for the way I acted. My past isn't your problem."

Mr. Woods set his cup down and rested his arms on the table.

"Son, I accept your apology, but part of the fault is mine. It's not proper to butt into someone else's business, but I worry about Kay. She's important to me, like my own daughter. She's lonely, and she's vulnerable. You understand my point, don't you?"

"Yes, sir, but I don't intend to hurt Kay."

"What are your intentions?"

Jake didn't answer right away. He wasn't sure about his feelings concerning Kay. He wasn't in love with her, but she had awakened emotions he thought long dead. Before he could answer, Mr. Woods continued.

"Her mother died of a heart attack ten years ago. Her dad, Amos Carter, died from cancer five years ago. Me and Amos were close. On his deathbed, he asked me to keep an eye on Kay. She was his pride and joy, and he wasn't going to be around for her. I promised I'd watch out for her as long as I'm alive." He grinned. "Now you know why I'm such a nosy old coot."

Jake debated his next question but felt he could trust the older man to be honest with him.

"Do you really believe I abandoned Marilyn all those years ago?"

Mr. Woods shrugged. "It's not important whether I believe it or not. But I'll tell you this much. When you left town, rumors flew thick and fast that you wouldn't be back. You were young and had a chance to get away from Archer Springs and try your wings. When Dale and Marilyn ran off, some said she married Summers on the rebound. Most didn't think it would last. But they surprised everyone by settling down and living together until young Monty graduated from high school."

It was true. His good intentions had been misinterpreted by the whole town. But why didn't Marilyn set them straight? Why didn't she wait for him?

SATURDAY EVENING, JUNE 12TH

The ringing phone jolted Marilyn Summers from her nap. She sat up, rubbed her eyes and reached for the receiver. "Hello."

"Hi, Mom."

"Hi, Monty. How are you?"

"I'm fine, Mom. It's Dad. He had another heart attack Thursday night. I would have called sooner, but I was waiting for his test results."

Monty's voice had a slight quaver to it, and Marilyn heard him take a deep breath. She knew he was worried.

"Thanks for letting me know. What does the doctor say about him?"

"He said it doesn't look good right now, but they're doing everything they can for him." Monty's voice broke, and he cleared his throat. "He doesn't look good to me."

Marilyn ran a hand through her hair, pushing stray strands away from her face. "Would you like me to come to Archer Springs?"

Monty sighed as if he'd been holding his breath while he talked to her. "That would be great. Thanks, Mom."

"I'll leave early in the morning. I should be there in time for breakfast."

They signed off, and Marilyn let out her own breath in a sigh. The thought of going to Archer Springs depressed her. Too many memories—old memories, but she knew Monty would feel better with her there. She went to the bedroom and started packing. She wondered if she should take something black, just in case, but pushed the thought away. No use being morbid.

Her suitcase packed, she headed to the kitchen for a snack. It was eight o'clock, and she hadn't eaten dinner. She needed to eat something light and go to bed so she could get up early for the drive to Archer Springs. She pulled salad fixings from the refrigerator just as the phone rang again.

"Hello?"

"Do you always answer on the first ring?" Kay asked.

Marilyn smiled. "I happened to be close by the phone. Funny you should call. I'm coming to Archer Springs."

"So you know about Dale then?"

"Yes. Monty called. He seemed anxious for me to come. Is it as bad as it sounds?"

"I'm afraid so," Kay said. "I've been debating about whether I should call you or not."

"I'll be there early in the morning. I plan to leave here around four."

She heard Kay take a deep breath on the other end of the line before she spoke. "There's something I think you should know before you get here."

"What is it?" A long pause followed, and an uneasy feeling crept over Marilyn.

"Jake's back."

Marilyn's heart leapt hard enough to make her lean against the kitchen counter for support. She felt as though someone had punched her in the stomach. She opened her mouth, but the words lodged in her throat.

"Marilyn, are you okay?"

She swallowed and tried to take a deep breath.

"Y-Yes, I'm fine," she lied. She couldn't let on how she felt. Not now. Not after all these years.

"You don't sound fine. I'm sorry, I guess I shouldn't have dumped this on you with Dale being so sick, but I thought you should know before you got here."

Marilyn closed her eyes. "How long has he been back?"

"He came this week. He's renovating the old home place on Orchard Street. I know this is difficult for you, but we can talk more when you get here."

Marilyn replaced the receiver and sat down at the kitchen table. Her racing heart hadn't slowed much, but at least she could breathe again.

What took you so long, Jake? I've been waiting all these years for you to come back. And now you show up.

One thing she knew for sure. He hadn't come back for her. Not after all this time. If he wanted her, he would have come home a long time ago.

CHAPTER 8

SUNDAY, JUNE 13TH

Dawn peeked over the horizon as Marilyn reached Archer Springs. A single question buzzed through her mind. How did Jake feel about her after all this time? Of course, he had the right to hate her, but maybe he didn't hold any hard feelings.

She was grateful for Kay's friendship. Marilyn knew when she married Dale that Kay would be hurt. As best friends, the two girls had shared everything, and Marilyn knew Kay was in love with Dale. Afterward, Kay wouldn't even acknowledge her when they met on the street or attended the same social events. Then she answered the doorbell one day to find Kay standing outside. Kay said she had come to ask for forgiveness because of a request from her father on his deathbed. He told Kay to ask God and Marilyn to forgive her for the bitterness she harbored. Marilyn had burst into tears. Their friendship had been restored that day.

When she reached the center of Archer Springs, she couldn't resist turning down Orchard Street. A pickup sat in the driveway of the old Reynolds house and someone stood on the front porch, coffee cup in hand. Marilyn's heart raced, and her hands trembled on the steering wheel.

Jake.

She couldn't see his face, but she knew it was him, and not because Kay had told her he had returned. For the first time in twenty-five years, she felt the magnetic pull she'd felt only when she was near him. She had never experienced it with anyone else, not even Dale, to whom she had been married for twenty years.

The man she truly loved had come home.

A patrol car stopped in front of the house as Jake finished adding the chain on the porch swing. The lanky, sandy-haired deputy who stepped out of the vehicle was the same young man who'd been on duty when he reported the fire.

The deputy nodded at Jake as he opened the gate and stepped into the yard.

"Morning, Mr. Reynolds." He stopped at the bottom of the porch steps and glanced over his shoulder as if looking for someone.

Jake looked in the same direction the deputy had indicated but the street was empty. "Is there a problem?"

"Could we talk inside?" He sounded nervous.

Jake shrugged. "Sure, come on in." He opened the door and they stepped into the living room.

"By the way, my name is Billy Wilson." He held out his hand, and they shook.

"What do you want to talk about?"

"Looks like you've already cleaned up the evidence of your fire," the younger man said, glancing around the room. "Can't prove much without it."

Jake nodded. "Yeah, but I didn't think anything would be done about the fire."

The deputy crossed his arms over his chest. "Why'd you think that?"

Jake ignored the question. "How about a soft drink? I could use one after working in the heat."

"Yeah, thanks, don't mind if I do." Billy pulled off his Stetson and wiped his brow. He followed Jake into the kitchen and sat at the table.

Jake pulled two drinks out of the ice chest and handed one to Billy.

"What's your real reason for coming here?" He sat down and opened his drink.

Billy popped the top on his can. "I didn't want you to think I'm not doing my job."

Jake didn't answer. He took a long swig of cola and pretended to stare out the back door. When he didn't respond, the younger man continued. "You're new in town, so you don't know how things are here in Archer Springs."

"I know enough to know I don't like it."

Billy sipped his drink and watched Jake over the top of his can. "I guess you've already met James Sheridan, then."

"Yes. He's one of the reasons I'm here." He shook his head at the questioning look on Billy's face. "It's a long story. I grew up here, but I left years ago. My aunt and uncle left me this property that your Mr. Sheridan wants to burn down."

Billy set his can down and propped his elbows on the table.

"Look, he's not my Mr. Sheridan. It's not right to force people out of their homes. It stinks as far as I'm concerned."

Jake drained his soft drink and crushed the aluminum can in his hand with one squeeze. "Someone needs to stop him."

Billy stared at the flattened can for a moment. "I wouldn't get any wild ideas about it if I were you."

"Isn't there anyone in town you can depend on for help?"

Billy held up his index finger. "One man. Right now, he's in the hospital with a heart attack. He's the only one I've seen stand up to Sheridan."

Jake knew without asking that Billy referred to Dale. It was Dale's no-fear attitude that had gotten them into all those scrapes when they were boys. He wasn't a smart aleck about it—he just wasn't afraid to stand his ground.

Billy sighed. "I'm the one person in the department who hasn't gotten his hands dirty with Sheridan's schemes."

"How have you managed that?"

"It isn't easy. So far I've been able to make myself unavailable every time he walks into the office, but one of these days I'll get caught." The deputy shook his head. "That'll be the day I lose my job. Until then, I'm going to do what I feel is right for the people of this town."

"And for some reason, you've decided you can trust me?"

"Anyone who isn't afraid to report an incident in this town and point a finger at the perpetrator is okay in my book." Billy sat back in his chair.

"What perpetrator?"

"You said a white Volkswagen left your house right after the fire. It belongs to Monty Summers."

"Why didn't you say so yesterday?"

"You're a stranger in town."

Jake blinked in surprise at the quick transition. "And now I'm not?"

"Old man Woods over at the motel thinks you're tops. If you're okay in his book, you're okay in mine."

"Are you going to arrest Monty Summers?"

Billy shook his head. "Can't. Not without hard evidence, and we don't have any. Besides, his old man is the one who isn't afraid of Sheridan. We can't afford to lose the one voice we have against the enemy."

He stood and walked to the front door. Jake tossed the flattened can on the table and followed him. "That's the end of it, then?"

Billy pushed open the screen door.

"It's important to me that people know I'm trying to do the right thing, and I wanted you to know I believe you. Thanks for the drink."

Jake stood on the porch and watched the young deputy drive away.

So now what? I sit by and let Sheridan burn down my house?

He shook his head.

No way.

Kay pushed her plate to one side and sipped her cranberry juice. Having breakfast ready when Marilyn arrived had been a wise idea. She looked at her friend sitting across the table, wondering how much she could handle.

Marilyn cleared her throat. "We've talked all around the subject, but you haven't mentioned Jake. What's he like after all this time?"

Kay set her glass down and took a deep breath. "In some ways, he's still the same old Jake, but he's also defensive and bitter."

Marilyn bit her lip but didn't say anything.

Kay smiled. "On the other hand, he's a good-looking man. And he still has a sense of humor—about some things, that is."

"Have you talked to him much?"

"Yes. I've been helping him paint the house, and we had dinner a few times." She noticed Marilyn's raised eyebrows. "Nothing special, just dinner, catching up for old time's sake."

Marilyn finished her waffle and reached for her coffee cup. "Is he married?"

Kay shook her head. "No."

"Has he mentioned me?"

"Your name has surfaced a few times." Kay traced the wood pattern in the table with her finger and debated the best way to make her next statement. "He won't visit Dale in the hospital."

"You told him about Dale's heart attack?"

Kay nodded. "Jake says he doesn't owe Dale anything. He's here because of his aunt's house, and he's had nothing but trouble because of it."

"What kind of trouble?"

"The Sheridan kind."

Marilyn frowned.

"James is still trying to get his hands on all the real estate in town?"

"Yes. Or he's burning it down if the owner won't sell, which Jake has refused to do."

"Why does that not surprise me?" Marilyn carried her plate to the sink, then leaned back against the counter. "Does Dale know Jake's in town?"

"Yes. He sent him a note, asking him to come for a visit." She watched Marilyn's face turn pale. Maybe she shouldn't have said anything about the note.

"Dale wants to see him?"

"Yes. He feels they need to settle the past."

Marilyn sighed. "What could he say that would change anything?"

Kay poured a little more cranberry juice into her glass and sipped it before answering.

"Dale wants to explain things to Jake. He wants to make peace with him."

"It's too late for that." Marilyn's eyes brimmed with tears. "We made our choices years ago. Now we have to live with the consequences."

Kay went to Marilyn and pulled her into a hug.

"It's Sunday. Go to church with me. It will do you good to sit with God for a while. You'll find the strength you need to face what's ahead."

Marilyn sighed. "If ever I needed strength, it's now. After all these years, I never thought Jake would come home."

SUNDAY AFTERNOON, JUNE 13

Ever since his arrival in Archer Springs, Jake knew he should make a trip to the cemetery to visit the graves of his Uncle George and Aunt Nora. They'd both died within two years of his leaving, and he'd never paid his respects.

As he walked to his pickup, thunder rumbled and large gray storm clouds loomed over head. A Texas thunderstorm would be a welcome gift right now.

As he backed out of the driveway, lightning streaked across the sky, and the scent of rain filled the air. He remembered what Kay had said about the drought for the past few years. Maybe this would be the break they all needed.

Archer Springs Memorial Cemetery sat one mile outside the city limits. His last visit here had been in 1954, when his grandfather Montcrief Reynolds had passed away. It had been a rough experience for a fifteen-year-old, who viewed his grandfather as the wisest man on earth, an invincible person who would always be there.

Jake parked the truck and walked in the direction of his grandfather's grave. At first he didn't see the family plot because so many markers had been added in the last twenty-five years. He spotted it hidden behind a towering stone angel and stopped to read the inscription on his grandfather's monument.

THOMAS MONTCRIEF REYNOLDS
BORN: JANUARY 3, 1867
DIED: APRIL 10, 1954
HE WAS A SHINING EXAMPLE FOR THOSE WHO KNEW HIM.
HE WILL BE MISSED.

Jake reached out to touch the worn stone marker.

I still miss you even after all these years. I wish you were here to help me make the right decisions now.

He swallowed the lump forming in his throat and straightened. Wishing wouldn't bring back the past. He knew that from experience. He glanced at a nearby marker. His grandmother had died when he was five years old. The mental images of her had almost disappeared. A cousin who died in infancy lay next to his grandmother. Jake sighed.

His parents should have been buried in this same plot, but he'd convinced them to move to Georgia years ago. When they realized he wasn't coming back to Archer Springs, they moved to a small town twenty-five miles from Atlanta. They were buried there.

A deafening clap of thunder made Jake flinch. The gray clouds he had noticed in town had turned black, and the wind tugged at his hair and clothes with greater intensity. Jake looked around for Aunt Nora's and Uncle George's graves. They were located a few feet away in a different plot. The big gray stone held both their names. As he knelt in front of the marker, the first drops of rain fell.

SARAH NORA BENTON REYNOLDS
BORN: AUGUST 12, 1892 ~ DIED: NOVEMBER 10, 1958
GEORGE BENTLEY REYNOLDS
BORN: OCTOBER 8, 1887 ~ DIED: JULY 21, 1959

Hot tears stung Jake's eyes. He knew why their deaths had occurred so close together. They had been so much in love that neither could survive without the other. Uncle George had often made the statement that he wouldn't want to live a single moment without his wife. Aunt Nora had died of a massive heart attack, and Uncle George had died of a massive broken heart.

Jake rubbed his hand across his eyes so he could read the rest of the inscription written beneath the names. The words seemed to leap at him from the stone surface.

"FOR IF YE FORGIVE MEN THEIR TRESPASSES, YOUR HEAVENLY FATHER WILL ALSO FORGIVE YOU: BUT IF YE FORGIVE NOT MEN THEIR TRESPASSES, NEITHER WILL YOUR FATHER FORGIVE YOUR TRESPASSES."
MATTHEW 6:14-15

Jake recoiled as if he had been slapped.

What a strange message for a cemetery marker.

As he stood at the stone, a bolt of lightning struck a tree in the field across the road. The tree exploded into flames. He looked back at the tombstone, and above the roar of the storm he could hear the inscription as though someone had spoken it aloud. He turned and hurried toward the pickup, the wind and rain whipping against his body.

He sat in the truck shivering, but he knew his wet clothes and skin weren't the cause. He could still hear those words reverberating in his head. He knew Aunt Nora. This was no coincidence. She was a godly woman who carried nothing in her heart against anyone. She'd chosen that verse for a reason. Had it been for him, hoping one day he would come home and forgive those who had wronged him?

James Sheridan tapped the end of his Mont Blanc pen on the stack of files in front of him. "What happened yesterday, Monty?"

Monty Summers fidgeted, shifting from one foot to the other. "Someone was inside the house."

"Well, maybe it's a good thing the fire didn't go as planned." A cynical grin crossed Sheridan's lips. "We don't want any bodies turning up in the ashes, do we?"

"No, sir." Perspiration formed on Monty's upper lip and trickled down his chin. "Would you like me to try again? I'll try to do a better job next time."

"Yes, I would." Sheridan tapped the files harder with his pen emphasizing each word as he spoke. "But don't try. Make sure you get it right this time. I want you as a fulltime employee, but I can't use you unless you can take orders and carry them out to the end."

"I will, sir. You can count on it."

Dale's chest rose and fell in a slow rhythm as his body took in the oxygen provided for him. All the color had left his face, and Marilyn noticed more gray in his jet-black hair. He looked older than the last time she'd seen him.

It had been almost a year since her last visit to Archer Springs. She encouraged Monty to come visit her when possible. It made things easier for all of them, not that she and Dale ever fought or argued. Their divorce, like their marriage, had been quiet and agreeable.

Dale stirred and opened his eyes. He blinked a few times and looked around. When he saw her, he smiled.

"Marilyn." He spoke in a ragged whisper. "I ... thought for a minute ... I was ... dreaming. But it *is* you."

She reached for his hand. The coldness of it surprised her. "Yes, it's me. How are you feeling?"

"Not good." His eyes traveled from her face to the clothes she wore. "You look beautiful as always."

She squeezed his hand. "Thank you."

His eyes searched her face.

"What is it?"

"Have you seen him?"

Marilyn swallowed and took a deep breath. "You mean Jake?"

"Yes."

"No." She let go of his hand and walked to the end of the bed. "Kay tells me you haven't seen him either."

"No." Dale sighed. "I asked him to come, but he hasn't yet."

She patted his foot. "Maybe it's best."

Dale shook his head. "There are things he needs to know."

Marilyn stared at the man lying in the bed. He had been a good husband. She was the one who had been unable to cope any longer. She wished she possessed his confidence and courage. "What good would it do any of us if you told him the truth? It will open old wounds, not to mention what it might do to Monty."

"Jake has a right to know we didn't betray him. Whether he forgives us or not, maybe he will find some closure. We owe him that much."

Marilyn fingered the edge of the blanket covering the bed. "Why now, after all these years? We did the only thing we could. The rest of our lives shouldn't be spent in regret. Besides, you of all people shouldn't feel any guilt."

"You can't tell me you haven't suffered because of this. I know you better than that."

Dale closed his eyes, and for a moment, she thought he had drifted off, until he spoke again.

"I want to die in peace, Marilyn."

His remark stunned her. Even though they were no longer married, she cared about him. Marilyn watched him for several minutes, but he didn't open his eyes again. His breathing eased as he slipped into sleep.

CHAPTER 9

Jake swallowed the last bite of toast and went to answer the knock at the door.

"Good morning," Kay said. "May I come in?"

He pushed open the screen door. "You look as though you could use some breakfast."

"That would be nice."

He led the way into the kitchen and pulled out a chair for her at the small table he'd borrowed from Mr. Woods. Kay smiled her thanks, but he noticed the smile didn't reach her eyes.

He set a cup of coffee in front of her and put more bread into the toaster. "Are you on your way to the hospital?"

"No. I came to talk to you."

"What about?"

She took a deep breath and added creamer to her coffee. "I don't know any other way to say this except to tell you point blank. Marilyn's in town. Monty called her about Dale."

He closed his eyes. The thing he'd dreaded most was happening. "Does she know I'm here?"

Kay lowered her head in apology.

"I know. I seem to be a self-appointed messenger." She reached over and touched his arm. "Please don't be angry with me. I felt she had the right to know, and I'm telling you for the same reason. I didn't want you running into each other by accident. Both of you are special to me, and I care about your feelings."

He frowned. "I guess I should say thanks, but at this point, I don't know if it's a good deed or a bad one."

She sipped her coffee. "Maybe it's time to get this whole thing out in the open and clear the air, so we can all be friends again and share what time Dale may have left."

Jake shook his head. "We can't change the past. It doesn't work that way."

"Well, we may not be able to do anything about the past, but we have another chance to make the future better for all of us. The four of us could spend some quality time together while you're in town."

He set his cup down.

"I appreciate all your peacemaking efforts, but what could the four of us have in common after all this time? What could we talk about? I don't want to hear how they spent their lives together the past twenty-five years. Besides, they made the decision to shut me out years ago."

The words from the tombstone echoed through his mind. *Forgive those who trespass against you.* He pushed the words away and sipped his coffee. It tasted bitter.

"I think they regret that decision now." Kay stood. "If you change your mind, would you call me?"

Jake followed her to the front door. "I won't change my mind."

She leaned over and brushed his cheek with her lips. "Whatever you decide, I'm still your friend."

"Thanks," he said. "Right now, I need every friend I can get."

Monty Summers set the Molotov cocktail on the kitchen table. Sadness crept over him. He had always liked that old house on Orchard Street. It had been one of his favorite childhood hideouts, ever since the summer he turned ten. He'd slipped in and walked through the rooms, wondering about the people who had lived there.

The house was cool inside in spite of the heat. He sat down in an old armchair full of holes and fell asleep. Sometime later, booming thunder woke him, and through the door he could see streaks of lightning racing across an angry sky. He didn't know why, but he felt safe inside the house, and he waited out the storm there. After that, whenever he wanted to be alone, he went to the house and hid out.

Now some guy had come to town, fixed up the old place, and moved in. Monty had been glad to see the house being renovated, until Sheridan decided it had to go. And you didn't argue with Sheridan. Anybody could make an anonymous phone call, spray red paint on walls, or toss a cocktail, but burning someone's house with them in it was different. He'd been raised to respect other people and their property. He knew his parents would be disappointed in him if they knew what he was doing, but once you involved yourself in Sheridan's schemes, he wouldn't let you out.

The doorbell interrupted his thoughts. He looked around at the paraphernalia on the table, then gathered it up and shoved it into one of the bottom cabinets. The doorbell rang again. He hurried to the front door and jerked it open.

"I was beginning to wonder if you were here."

"Hi, Mom." Monty hugged her, and she kissed him on the cheek. "How come you rang the bell? Don't you still have a key?"

Marilyn shook her head. "I gave it to your dad on my last visit here." She wrinkled her nose and sniffed the air. "It smells funny in here. Is that gasoline? What are you doing, Monty, trying to burn the house down?"

CHAPTER 10

TUESDAY EVENING, JUNE 15TH, 8:00 P.M.

Jake sat at the kitchen table and munched on a bologna and cheese sandwich. After the delicious food at Garrett's Diner, cold cuts made for a boring meal. He hadn't heard from Kay since the day before when she broke the news to him about Marilyn, so he'd opted to go shopping and pick up something easy.

Shoving the last bite into his mouth, he grabbed a soda from the ice chest in the corner and headed for the front porch. He sat in the swing and took a big swig of soda. The outdoors was cooler than a house without air conditioning, even though the temperature hadn't dropped much after the first stars of evening appeared. He pushed against the porch with one foot to start the swing moving—anything to stir up a little breeze. Then above the porch swing chain's rhythmic squeak, he heard a car engine.

When the white Volkswagen rounded the corner, the muscles in his neck tightened. As the car crept toward the house, Jake noticed the driver's hand at the window, clutching an object. A light, like the small flame of a cigarette lighter, glowed deeper inside the car. As the car reached the driveway, Jake stood and walked to the edge of the porch. The driver jerked his hand back inside and accelerated, but not before Jake saw the familiar ponytail hanging down his back.

Pulling the keys from his pocket, he ran to his own vehicle and jumped in. He backed out of the drive, tires squealing, and then stomped the accelerator and headed in the Volkswagen's direction. As he rolled down the streets of Archer Springs, he wondered what he would do to the Summers kid if he did catch him. Jake searched the area for several minutes, but car and driver had vanished. He slammed his fist against the steering wheel and headed for the sheriff's office.

Billy Wilson looked up as Jake stormed through the door. "Hi, Jake. What brings you here?"

Jake leaned over the counter and glared at Billy. "A white Volkswagen and a guy with a ponytail."

The deputy frowned. "Trouble again, huh?"

"The lowlife was planning to throw another Molotov cocktail. When he saw me, he jerked his hand back inside the car." Jake's hands curled into fists. "I want to know what you're going to do about it."

Billy glanced around the office and lowered his voice.

"We've already been through this." He picked up a pen, and his voice returned to normal. "Now, Mr. Reynolds, tell me what happened."

Jake continued to glare at Billy but told him the details.

"So nothing happened, did it?" Billy asked. "You're assuming he was going to throw the object." He shook his head. "I'm sorry, Jake. There's nothing we can do."

Jake slapped the counter with the palm of his hand, then shook his finger in Billy's face. "Somebody better get this problem under control, or I'm going to do something about it myself."

Billy held up both hands in surrender but lowered his voice to a whisper. "Hey, now don't go doing anything stupid. You know the situation around here."

Jake took a deep breath, then exhaled.

"I can't believe no one's standing up to Sheridan. Why is this whole blasted town letting him get away with this?"

Billy tapped the ballpoint pen against the countertop, lowering his voice again. "You already know the answer to that."

Jake stared at the young deputy for several seconds. "That doesn't make me like it any better." He knew Billy couldn't do anything about Sheridan. There wasn't any need in getting mad at the kid. He spun and walked toward the door.

"Jake."

He looked back at the deputy.

Billy glanced over his shoulder before speaking. "Maybe you should go see Sheridan yourself. Try to work out a deal, since you're not a permanent resident here. Don't do anything crazy."

Jake nodded. "Yeah, I think you're right. But I'm not looking forward to it."

Monty leaned back against the headrest in the Volkswagen and closed his eyes. Another close call. And this time he'd been seen. He put his trembling hand over his heart, wishing it would slow down. He wasn't cut out for this kind of thing. He didn't like burning houses or threatening people. So far, he was guilty of making a threatening phone call and spray painting the house on Orchard, but burning a house and possibly injuring or killing someone would be a bigger sentence. He would tell Sheridan to count him out. He didn't want to disappoint his dad, but that might be better than what had almost happened tonight. If he'd lit the firebomb and thrown it, the man might have been killed.

Darkness descended around him and he felt safer. Monty switched on the ignition and pulled out of the alley, checking to make sure the way was clear. When he reached James Sheridan's office, he parked behind the building and knocked on the back entrance. Sheridan opened the door.

"Come in, Monty." He smiled. "Do you have good news for me?"

Monty stepped into the office, his body still trembling.

Sheridan rubbed his hands together in anticipation. "Well, out with it. What happened?"

Monty tried to keep his voice steady, but it still squeaked. "I ... I'm sorry, Mr. Sheridan. I can't do this."

Sheridan's eyes flickered and his expression changed. A look cold enough to freeze the sun passed across his face. The muscle in his right cheek twitched.

"What do you mean, you can't do this?"

Monty shook his head. "I can't burn people's houses while they're living there."

Sheridan's face changed from bright pink to fiery red. It reminded Monty of fire leaping to life in a pile of tinder. Fear crept up Monty's back, and its fingers curled around his throat. He'd seen Sheridan's temper boil out of control more than once, and when it did, someone always got hurt.

"What do you mean, you can't burn houses? There's nothing to it. You strike a match and up it goes." Sheridan laughed. "Or maybe I should say down it goes. How hard can that be?"

Monty looked at the floor. His athletic shoes looked cheap and dirty on the thick, expensive carpet.

"It's not right, sir. I don't want any part of it."

Sheridan walked over and sat down behind the desk. "Tell you what, Monty. I like you, so I'm going to give you one more chance."

Monty could tell Sheridan was fighting to keep his anger under control. He shook his head.

"N-n-no, thanks." He managed to look at Sheridan when he said the words, but his knees knocked so hard he thought he might collapse.

The muscle in the side of Sheridan's jaw twitched again.

"You know, your dad won't be happy to hear about your little escapades."

Sweat trickled down Monty's face and neck, inside his shirt and down his chest.

"Please leave my dad out of it. I don't want him to worry about me. He's too sick."

"Then I think you'd better reconsider your position here. I can't let you off that easy. You know too much."

Monty didn't like the implication of the other man's words, but he couldn't commit murder. He cleared his throat and attempted to still his quivering lips.

"I've already considered it ... and I'm not going to do it."

Sheridan opened one of the desk drawers. "Then you leave me no choice."

Monty turned and started for the doorway.

"Nobody walks out on me." Sheridan's voice smoldered with anger.

Monty heard a click and glanced over his shoulder. When he saw the gun, he jumped for the door and jerked it open. As he did, a hammer blow hit him in the back. He stumbled and nearly fell, but managed to stay on his feet and scramble away.

Outside, Monty reached for the handle on the car door but couldn't hold onto it. He fell, his fingernails scratching across the white metal. He raised up and reached for the handle again, gripping it with every ounce of strength he had left. The door opened, and he struggled to pull himself into the car but succeeded only in falling across the seat. Unable to hold on, he slid back and slumped onto the ground beside the vehicle. Pain flooded his body, and he heard the racing of a rapidly moving car before the darkness came for him.

CHAPTER 11

Just as Jake raised his hand to bang on the locked office door of Sheridan Construction, a gunshot shattered the quiet. He flinched and ducked. After a few seconds he didn't feel any pain, so the shooter had either missed him or wasn't aiming for him.

Jake ran down the sidewalk to the alley that led behind the building. As he stepped around the corner, a car bore down on him. He flattened himself against the building as the car tore past, and instinctively he bellowed at the fading taillights.

"Crazy idiot!"

He moved silently across the parking area, looking for anything suspicious. When he spotted the white Volkswagen, he picked up his pace.

As he stealthily rounded the vehicle, he stumbled and almost fell over a body lying beside the car. In the streetlamp's dim light, he noticed the ponytail. *Monty Summers.* He knelt beside the body, and the metallic odor of blood rose to meet him.

He felt for a pulse and detected a faint response.

"Monty, can you hear me?" He took hold of Monty's shoulder to turn him over and felt something warm, wet, and sticky.

He raced to the nearest office door and turned the knob. Incredibly, it was open.

"Hello, anybody here? We need help." He stepped inside and looked around the deserted office. He grabbed the telephone and dialed 9-1-1.

After giving the operator his location, Jake hurried back to Monty. It looked like he'd lost an awful lot of blood, maybe too much.

Billy Wilson repeated the question a second time.

"Did you shoot Monty?"

Jake let out an exasperated sigh.

"No. I already told you. I found him in the alley behind Sheridan's office. I don't even own a gun." He closed his eyes and leaned across the desk. "You should be talking to Sheridan. Do we really have to go over this again?"

Billy shook his head.

"I'm sorry, Jake, but you were here less than two hours ago making threats. I have to check out all the possibilities."

"You're the one who suggested I go talk to Sheridan."

"I know." Billy stood. "Okay. Thanks for your help. I may need to talk to you again later, so don't leave town without notifying me."

Jake rolled his eyes at Billy and shut the door a little harder than necessary. He hated the thought of going home alone. Finding the body had unnerved him. He left the sheriff's office and drove to Kay's house, relieved to see Marilyn's car wasn't in the drive.

Kay answered the door. A smile lit her face when she saw him.

"Jake, come in. What a nice surprise."

He leaned against the doorframe and took a deep breath, willing himself to calm down so he could tell her what had happened.

She gasped. "There's blood on your shirt. Are you hurt?"

He shook his head. "I'm fine. Monty Summers has been shot."

"Oh, no. Oh, dear God, no." A look of horror crossed her face, and her eyes filled with tears. "How did it happen? Are you sure it was Monty?"

He slipped his arm around her as much to comfort himself as to support her. "I'm sure. I'm the one who found him."

Kay leaned against him, her body trembling. "How did it happen?"

"I don't know. I went to Sheridan's office to confront him. I heard a gunshot, and then I found Monty in the alley behind the office. I have a feeling Sheridan had something to do with it."

Tears slid down her cheeks. "Is he ...?"

"Dead? Not when I found him. He'd lost a lot of blood by the time the ambulance came." His head dropped. "They've had me at the sheriff's office answering questions for the last hour."

Kay wiped at her face. "Why were they questioning you? Surely they don't think you did it?"

He ran a hand through his hair. "I don't think so, but I happened to be the one to find him, so they might be a little suspicious."

"Oh, no." She put her hand on her throat. "I wonder if Marilyn knows about it. I've got to find her. She's going to need me."

She started for the door, then stopped and looked around the room, confusion written across her face.

"Where're my purse and keys?" She glanced around frantically, then covered her face with her hands and started sobbing again.

Jake pulled her into his arms, and she buried her face against his chest. "Maybe I better drive you to the hospital."

She nodded. "Thank you."

Ten minutes later, Jake pulled in front of the big double doors and waited for Kay to get out.

She reached for the door handle. "Aren't you coming in?"

He shook his head. "I don't belong in there. Marilyn has enough to deal with without me showing up."

She looked at him as if she wanted to say something, but instead stepped out of the car and shut the door.

He watched her hurry up the stone steps before he drove away.

Marilyn Summers wiped at the flood of tears streaming down her face. Useless! She couldn't stop the flow any more than she could shake off the dark fear threatening to swallow her. She walked to the door of the surgery waiting area and searched the hall again, a process she had repeated every five minutes for the last half hour.

How could this happen?

She had asked herself the same question a dozen times since the sheriff's deputy arrived at Dale's house looking for her. How he'd known to come there, she didn't know. She had gone over to visit with Monty, but he had plans for the early evening. After he left, promising to return soon, she'd started cleaning the house, just for something to do. Then the deputy showed up at the door.

"Marilyn." Kay hurried toward her. A fresh torrent of tears spilled down her face.

"Oh, Kay, Monty's been shot."

Marilyn collapsed into Kay's open arms. Kay led them to two empty chairs, and they sat and clung to each other in the empty waiting room.

After a few moments, Marilyn raised her head. "How did you know I was here?"

"Jake told me."

Marilyn leaned back out of Kay's embrace. "How did he know?"

Kay held Marilyn's hands in hers.

"Jake found Monty. He went to Sheridan's office to confront him, but he heard a gun go off, and he found Monty shot in the alley behind the office."

Marilyn's voice caught in her throat. "Do they know each other? Jake and Monty?"

"No, but he knows Monty is your son."

Marilyn stood and paced to the doorway again.

"What's taking them so long?"

Kay went to her side and slipped her arm around her shoulders. "I'm sure they'll tell us as soon as they know anything."

Marilyn shook her head.

"They can't let him die. He's all I've got."

CHAPTER 12

Marilyn rose as the doctor strode through the surgery suite doors and walked toward her. Kay joined her and slipped her arm around Marilyn's waist.

"How is he?"

"We've run into a problem," Dr. Ashworth said.

"What kind of a problem?" Fear rose in the pit of Marilyn's stomach. "Is it bad?"

Dr. Ashworth cleared his throat.

"We were able to extract the bullet. It missed his vital organs, but it nicked several large blood vessels. He's lost a lot of blood, and we're in a bind with getting him the blood he needs."

Marilyn visibly paled.

"You're his mother," the doctor said, "so you know his blood type is AB negative. It's an uncommon type in this area."

Marilyn worked to stifle the fear hovering around her. "Don't you have any blood here to give him?"

"We did," Dr. Ashworth said. "We gave him the one unit of AB negative we had on hand, and we've given him most of our Rh negative blood supply, plus other fluids to maintain his blood pressure. The problem is that he's used all the blood we can give him. He's stable right now, but we still need at least one more unit, possibly two, to have on hand until we're sure he's out of danger."

"Can't you get it from somewhere else? Some other hospital?" Marilyn's fear was audible in her voice, and Kay took her arm to steady her.

The doctor nodded.

"We've got some on the way from Amarillo, but that's two and a half hours from here, and they're having rough weather between here and there. Several tornadoes have touched down in the area, and they're waiting to see if they can transport it safely."

Both Marilyn and Kay stared at him, stunned into silence.

"The point," Dr. Ashworth continued, "is that we need at least one more unit for backup while we wait for the shipment. We don't routinely draw units of blood here and then give them to patients, because normally a lot of pre-transfusion testing for communicable diseases is done on blood units, and a lot of paperwork would be involved. But in this instance—"

"Oh, *please*," Marilyn cried, clinging to Kay's arm. "Can't you do it this once?"

Dr. Ashworth took her by the shoulders.

"Listen to me carefully. You'll have to sign a release saying that you understand the risks Monty will face if he's given unscreened blood. He may end up with syphilis or hepatitis, possibly other diseases. Are you willing to accept that responsibility for him?"

"Yes." Her answer was immediate and firm.

"Then we'll need to find an AB negative donor of the right age and in good health who is able—and willing—to tolerate having a pint of blood drawn. Your husband can't donate, because he's just down the hall in ICU and in no shape to give blood. We've asked around the hospital here, but no one fits the bill or knows any AB negative folks they could call on."

Marilyn was silent, her mind racing down a road of memories toward an unescapable conclusion. There was someone in town with Monty's type.

Jake.

"Dr. Ashworth?" The nurse's voice came from the surgery suite door. "Monty Summers is out of Recovery and in ICU."

"Can I see him?" Marilyn asked.

The doctor nodded to the nurse in acknowledgment, then turned to Marilyn. "You can go in for only a minute."

She followed the doctor down the hall to ICU. Outside the door, Dr. Ashworth turned to her.

"Let me go in and check his vitals, and make sure he's not sprung a leak somewhere." He gave her a tired smile. "He's one lucky young man. Don't stay too long."

He disappeared through the ICU doors, and Marilyn waited until a nurse came to the door and beckoned to her.

Marilyn slipped inside the unit and stared at Monty's pale face, almost invisible underneath all the tubes and tape. She reached for his hand, then laid the back of her other hand against his cheek. The only sound in the room was the swoosh of the ventilator breathing for him, and the rustle of a nurse tech who came in briefly to check the machine's settings.

Fresh tears threatened to surface. She bit her lip and forced them back. She had to be strong for both Monty and Dale.

She couldn't imagine life without her child. Marilyn closed her eyes. *Thank you, God, for allowing my son to live. Please help us to get the blood he needs before it's too late.*

A nurse took Monty's pulse and glanced at the monitor display screen with its pulsating lines. Marilyn watched her face for an encouraging sign, but she only nodded and left.

Marilyn leaned over and brushed Monty's forehead with her lips, then closed her eyes and breathed silent prayers as she held his hand in hers. She remained in that position until the doctor touched her arm.

"Marilyn, why don't you try and get some rest?"

She took one last look at Monty, then slipped outside.

Dr. Ashworth followed her out. "I thought you might like to know we've moved Dale to a private room. I felt the stress of his son being in ICU with him would be too much, even though he's stronger now and doing better. I know this is rough on you. Try and keep your chin up." He patted her arm. "And pray."

Marilyn entered the empty waiting room and sank onto a chair. So many unbelievable things happening at the same time. Dale's heart attack. Monty getting shot. Jake's return. What did it all mean? Had the past caught up with her? She buried her face in her hands as sobs shook her body.

"Marilyn, is Monty okay?" Kay stood over her with two cups of coffee.

"No, nothing new. The doctor says he's stable." She dug in her purse for a tissue and wiped her eyes, then accepted the coffee.

Kay sat next to her. "Is there anything I can do?"

Marilyn nodded and reached for her friend's hand.

"Pray for Monty and for a blood donor. It may be the only thing that saves him."

CHAPTER 13

Jake filled the coffeemaker with water and measured out grounds. While it brewed, he opened his breakfast of a package of bagels and a carton of cream cheese. While he ate, he considered the events of the previous night, and hoped Monty Summers was okay, despite his crimes. A knock at the door interrupted his thoughts, and he stuffed the last bite in his mouth before he went to greet his caller.

Kay stood on the front porch, her eyes swollen and red, clothes rumpled. She tried to smile, but exhaustion clouded her usual cheery countenance.

"May I come in?"

"Of course." Jake held the door for her. "Have you been at the hospital all night?"

She nodded. "I'm going home for a shower and a nap. I couldn't get Marilyn to leave. She insists on staying with Monty, even though she can't be in the room with him all the time."

"Then he's alive."

"Yes." She stood on her tiptoes and hugged him. "The doctor said if he hadn't been brought in when he was, he wouldn't have made it. Thank you, Jake."

He shrugged. "I didn't do anything but make a call."

Kay sank onto the sofa. "Yes, but I know how you feel about him. Thank you for putting those feelings aside to help Monty."

Jake frowned as he sat down on the other end of the sofa.

"In spite of what you might think of me, I do respect other people. Besides, I can't hold something against the kid that his parents are responsible for. On the other hand, he's playing with fire himself, in more ways than one."

"Marilyn's grateful for what you did."

"I would have done it for anyone. I'm not so hardhearted I'd let someone die."

"I know, but in light of the circumstances, I'm thankful for what you did."

"Is he going to make it?"

Kay sighed, and her eyes misted over.

"He's stable for now, but the doctor said he lost a lot of blood. He needs a transfusion. I hope they find a donor soon."

"What do you mean? Doesn't the hospital have blood they can give him?"

"Monty has a rare type, and they've contacted their blood supplier, but what with bad weather in their area and being two and a half hours away, that may not be an option right now. You know how isolated we are. The hospital is asking anyone with AB negative blood to come in and donate."

The hair on the back of Jake's neck stood up, and he broke out in a sweat.

"Are you okay, Jake?"

He glanced at Kay and found her staring at him. "Yes. Why do you ask?"

"You're pale."

He forced himself to smile. "I'm fine. You're the one who needs to get some rest."

She stood and stifled a yawn with her hand. "I'm going to do that right now, but I need a favor. One of the nurses dropped me here on her way home. Think you could give me a lift?"

"Of course." He followed her outside, still thinking about Monty. How could the kid have the same blood type as he did? Unless Monty was ...

He immediately dropped that line of thought.

I come back here to keep a promise, and I end up involved in all kinds of trouble. Just my luck.

By the time he returned from taking Kay home, the coffee was ready, and Jake took a fresh cup out to the porch. He sat in the swing, arguing with his conscience about donating blood for the Summers kid. He didn't notice Mr. Malone walking toward the house until the older man spoke.

"Howdy, Jake." Mr. Malone opened the gate and let himself inside the yard. He ambled to the porch and sat on the top step.

"Morning. Want a cup of coffee?"

"Thanks, but I've had my morning's allowance."

Jake remained in the porch swing. They sat in silence for a few moments, enjoying the quietness.

Malone pushed his straw hat farther back on his head. "I heard about young Summers. You're the one found him, they say."

"Yes." The Archer Springs grapevine was obviously in good working order, having already spread the news.

"Folks are saying you saved his life."

Jake didn't respond. He wondered where the conversation was leading.

Mr. Malone turned to look at him. "That's a step toward peace."

"What does that have to do with peace?"

"A fella doesn't reach out to someone he dislikes unless he wants to establish peace." Malone rubbed his chin. "The way I figure it, you've got a little pride standing in your way."

"You're wrong," Jake said. "I did what any decent human would have done. It didn't mean anything."

Malone swatted at a fly buzzing around his head.

"I understand they need blood donors with a rare type." He turned and looked at Jake. Their eyes locked. "What's your blood type?"

Jake hesitated a moment before lying. "A-positive."

Malone stared at Jake, who felt as though the old man could see right through him. He looked out across the yard, wondering if Malone knew he'd lied.

"Well," Malone finally said, without taking his eyes off Jake, "that lets you off the hook. I'd give young Summers some blood myself, if I had the right kind. You know there's no greater sacrifice than one man giving life to another."

"I did my part last night." Jake didn't mean to sound cold, but he knew it came out that way.

The old man nodded.

"Yes. I suppose you did." He took off his straw hat and fanned himself. "Have you thought any more about going to see Dale Summers?"

The fly had moved to Jake's space now. He swatted at it in frustration. "I don't think it's a good idea."

"For who? You or Summers?"

His coffee had grown cold. Jake flung the rest of it into the yard. "Neither one of us."

Once again Malone turned and looked Jake in the eyes.

"What are you afraid of, son?"

Jake gritted his teeth. "I'm not afraid of anything. I don't feel I owe him."

They sat without speaking for the next few minutes. It wasn't even ten o'clock yet, but the temperature had already moved into the nineties. Bees and yellow jackets buzzed in the yard, lit in the dry grass, then darted off again, looking for more succulent feasts.

After a few minutes, Mr. Malone stood and ambled back down the walk. At the gate, he turned.

"Face your fears, Jake. Swallow your pride. You'll win in the end."

WEDNESDAY, JUNE 16TH, 7:00 P.M.

Marilyn stretched out on the sofa in the hospital waiting room, ignoring all suggestions to go home and get some rest. She was exhausted, but she wanted to be near Monty in case of any change. She closed her eyes. Memories from the past flooded her mind. One in particular stood out—the day she realized she was pregnant.

All the signs had been there—the missed period, the nausea, the loss of energy. She'd gone to see Jake's Aunt Nora.

"Have you heard from Jake since he left?"

Nora Reynolds frowned. "Why no, child. I'd think you'd be the first to hear anything out of that boy."

"He's called a couple of times, but not in the past few days." Marilyn bit her lip, fighting back tears. "I wish he would call. I need to talk to him."

Nora patted Marilyn's arm. "I'm sure he's in a wheat field somewhere with no phone for miles. Don't worry, dear, he'll call, first chance he gets."

Marilyn returned home, fear rising in her throat, wondering how long she would be able to keep her secret.

The next day, the nausea came in waves. Her mother, thinking she had a virus, sent her back to bed for the day. Marilyn got up the following morning determined to appear normal, but the sickness took its toll again, and every day thereafter for the rest of the week.

On Saturday, her mother came into her room and sat on the edge of the bed. She brushed Marilyn's hair back from her forehead and laid her hand against the girl's cheek.

"I'm going to ask you something, and I want a straight answer."

Marilyn knew what was coming and closed her eyes, wanting to shut out the question.

"I thought you had a virus, but I suspect it's more than that. Are you in trouble?"

Marilyn lay there wondering how to answer the question. How could she tell her parents she was carrying Jake's child? They were proud people. Her mother had taken her to church since she was small, and her father, though not a religious man, ruled his household with a rod of iron.

Her mother reached out and touched her on the shoulder.

"Marilyn, are you pregnant?"

Marilyn opened her eyes as tears rolled down her cheeks. "I'm sorry, Momma."

Her mother blinked back her own tears and sighed. "Is Jake the father?"

Marilyn nodded. A fresh wave of nausea rolled over her. She hurried to the bathroom as the bile rose in her throat. Afterwards, she sat on the bathroom floor, shame and misery consuming her, not wanting to see the look on her mother's face again.

That night, Marilyn decided to try to eat. When she sat down at the table and saw her father's expression, she knew her mother had told him.

He waited until they finished the meal before he tossed his napkin on the table and glared at her.

"How could you bring such shame on this family?" His voice dripped with contempt.

Marilyn tried to swallow. Her mouth felt stuffed with cotton. She reached for her tea glass, but her hand shook and she spilled the drink on her skirt.

"I asked you a question, girl. I expect an answer."

"I ... I'm sorry," she stammered, wiping her wet clothes with the towel her mother had brought her.

"Look at me when I'm talking to you," he shouted, and slapped the table with both hands. "Is that all you have to say for yourself? You're sorry?" Her father stood. "Is this Jake Reynolds's doing?"

Marilyn nodded, tears sliding down her cheeks.

"And he's not even here to make an honest woman out of you." Her father spit the words like venom. "Does he know about this?"

Marilyn brushed at the tears. "N-n-no. I haven't heard from him."

"And you won't." Her father hit the palm of his hand with his fist. "Good thing he's not here. I'd beat the life out of him. He's—run—off—*and—he-ain't—coming—back*."

Marilyn leaned back in the chair and closed her eyes, her strength gone, drained away with her tears. The smell of the food nauseated her, and her father's anger made it worse.

"Only one solution to this problem," her father said, his words biting the air. "Get rid of it."

The words shot through her like hot acid. She screamed and jumped to her feet.

"*No!*"

Her father's hands curled into fists, wrinkling the tablecloth.

"Don't raise your voice to me, young lady. You'll do as I say."

Marilyn knew she should keep quiet, but the reality of what her father was saying overwhelmed her. "You can't do that. *I* can't do that. It's not right."

"I'm not having any daughter of mine living in this house with her bastard baby."

She shrank from his harsh words.

"I'll go away somewhere, where no one knows me."

"And do what? You got no money, no job. Ain't no close kin for you to stay with." He shook his head. "I'll talk to Doc Ashworth. He'll know somebody who can take care of it."

Marilyn opened her mouth to protest, but her father held up his hand.

"No. It's settled. I've made my decision."

Marilyn ran to her room and fell across her bed. She cried until she fell asleep, exhausted. She woke in the middle of the night, still in her clothes. She sat on the side of the bed and looked out the window. A full moon had risen. She moved to the window and knelt on the floor, looking out at the star-littered sky.

Jake, where are you? I need you. I can't let Daddy take this baby from me. It belongs to us.

Over the next few days, she waited to hear from Jake. She kept hoping to open the door one day and find him standing on the porch, but he didn't show. Her father didn't mention her predicament again, but Marilyn knew he hadn't forgotten. She could tell by his look and worse, his silence. She avoided him, staying in her room most of the time.

Then one night at supper, he broke the news.

"I've found someone to get rid of our problem." He spooned gravy onto his mashed potatoes as if he was speaking about killing rats in the cellar. "Your appointment is tomorrow."

"No!" Her chair tipped over and bounced over the floor as she jerked to her feet.

"It's already been arranged," her father said, without looking up.

"You can't do this," she said. "It makes you a murderer."

Her father moved faster than she could react. In one lightning-smooth motion he rose and pulled his arm back as he shifted his weight for more power. Then he leaned over the table and hit her full in the face. His slap knocked her off her feet, and she fell backward into the legs of her toppled chair and from there onto the floor. Her mother ran to her, but Marilyn wrenched away, struggled to her feet, and raced out the front door.

She ran until her throat and lungs burned. She slowed and continued to walk, ending up on the opposite side of town. Her head and face throbbed. She tasted blood. A car honked, but she was afraid to turn around and look, for fear the sheriff had been sent for her. Or worse—her father had tracked her down.

"Hey, where you going? Want a lift?"

The familiar voice made her look up and then hurry to the car and open the door. When the dome light came on and Dale caught a glimpse of her face, he uttered a curse.

"What on earth happened to you? Your nose is bleeding. You've got blood on your blouse. Get in!"

Marilyn tried to swallow the painful lump in her throat, but all she could do was shake her head while tears streamed down her face.

Dale drove to Malone's drive-in and parked.

"Marilyn, tell me what happened. Who did this to you?" He swore again. "Jake will kill me when he finds out. He asked me to keep an eye on you while he's gone." He put his finger under Marilyn's chin and lifted her face until he could see her eyes. "Did someone attack you?"

Marilyn turned away and looked out the window.

"My dad—" She gulped. "My dad hit me."

Dale punched the steering wheel with his fist. "Why?"

She looked away from him, shame flooding through her. "I'm pregnant."

Dale whistled through his teeth.

"Jiminy cricket, Marilyn." He turned and looked out the window for a moment, then back at her. "Is it Jake's?"

She nodded and told him about her father and his plans.

"I can't go back home. If I do, he'll force me to get rid of it." Fresh tears rolled down her face. "I want this baby."

"Can you get in touch with Jake?"

Marilyn shook her head. "They're moving around too much. He calls me when he gets near a phone, but sometimes it's several days between calls."

The rest of the conversation was a blur until Dale threw her the bombshell.

"I think we should get married."

She stared at him, wondering if she'd heard right. "Are you crazy?"

He shrugged as if he proposed marriage every day.

"We get married. I'll say the baby's mine. That way your old man can't kill it."

123

She shook her head.

"Daddy knows it's Jake's baby." She put her hand on her stomach. "I can't. I can't marry you. You know I love Jake."

He shook his head.

"Seems to me you don't have a whole lot of choices. Jake's not due home for two months. Meanwhile, what happens to his child? I promised him I'd watch out for you. I guess now that includes his kid too."

Marilyn felt like she would be sick right then and there in Dale's car. She knew what would happen if she didn't go along with Dale's solution. Her father would force her to have an illegal abortion.

"What about Jake and all our plans?"

"Look," Dale said, "when Jake comes home, we'll get a divorce, or—what do they call it?—an annulment. I'll talk to my dad. He'll arrange it. He won't like it, but he'll help us."

Marilyn shook her head. "Your folks aren't going to like this any more than mine."

Dale cupped her chin with his hand and turned her face toward him.

"What's more important to you at this point? What our parents think, or the life of your child? Besides, you know I'd do anything for Jake."

"I know. You two are closer than brothers, but there's also the fact that divorce isn't acceptable in the church. We'll be outcasts."

Dale shrugged. "I know, but we don't have a choice if you want to keep this baby."

Marilyn didn't go home that night. Dale took her to a local motel and paid for a room so she'd have a place to sleep. She spent the night praying, asking God and Jake to forgive her. The next day they drove to Austin, where they found a justice of the peace.

In the hospital waiting room outside ICU, Marilyn shivered at the memory and sat up. The decision she and Dale had made that night still filled her with regret and a longing for what might have been different, except for one thing. She had a son whom she loved. If she'd listened to her father twenty-five years ago, there would be no Monty.

Maybe this was her punishment for the things she'd done in the past. Maybe God had waited all this time to make her pay for her sin.

CHAPTER 14

Marilyn flipped through the pages of a worn copy of *Ladies' Home Journal.* She had read every article as well as the ads. The only other magazines on the waiting room table were *Farm and Ranch* and *Texas Highways.* She stood and wandered to the window. Sunlight streamed through the window. It had been a long night.

"Good morning, Marilyn."

She turned at the doctor's voice.

"I wanted to let you know Monty is still holding his own, but I don't know for how long." He patted Marilyn's arm. "We're doing everything we can for him. If he was in better condition, I'd have him moved to a larger facility, but he's still too weak. And too, there's the situation with the weather. Lots of damage between here and Amarillo."

Marilyn hugged the older man. "You've always taken such good care of us. Ever since Monty's birth."

The old doctor rubbed his red, sleep-deprived eyes and smiled. "I'm glad you didn't abort that boy all those years ago. Your daddy and I had an awful fight about that, you know."

"No. I didn't know."

"I was younger than your daddy, hadn't been out of medical school too many years. When he approached me about terminating your pregnancy, I told him I didn't want anything to do with it. I'd taken an oath to preserve life, not take it. It was 1957, and in those days, abortion was illegal." He sighed and ran his hand through his gray hair. "I wouldn't have done it even if it had been legal, but your daddy was bent on, as he put it, 'getting rid of the disgrace.' He threatened me."

Marilyn frowned. The old resentment toward her dad surfaced.

"What kind of threat?"

"He said if I didn't help him find someone to get rid of your problem, he'd see to it I'd never practice in this state again."

"How could he do that? You hadn't done anything wrong."

"A few years before, during my internship, I misdiagnosed a woman's condition and gave her the wrong medication." Dr. Ashworth sighed again. "She had a reaction to the medicine and slipped into a coma. She finally recovered, but the incident has haunted me since then. When her family didn't file a suit, I came back here to practice, and somehow your daddy found out about the incident. Anyway, I made inquiries, until I found someone who would do the abortion." He squeezed her hand and smiled. "You can't imagine the relief I felt when I heard you and Dale had eloped."

"I'm sorry, Dr. Ashworth. I had no idea Daddy threatened you."

The doctor shook his head. "No need to be sorry, Marilyn. He thought he was protecting his family from what would be certain ruin. In those days, unwed mothers were considered a disgrace. Things have changed since then. Not much for the better, I might add." After a moment, he smiled. "I'm proud of you and the decision you made every time I see Monty."

Marilyn reached out and squeezed his hand.

"Thank you for standing up for me, even though I was a kid. I don't know what I would have done if Dale hadn't married me."

"By the way, I looked in on Dale a few minutes ago."

"Any change?"

"Still not good, but better than yesterday." He laid his hand on Marilyn's shoulder. "I wouldn't mention Monty's condition to him if I were you. I know this is hard on you, but I think we should give him a little more time to recover."

Marilyn knew she needed to visit Dale. She'd been so consumed with Monty's situation that she had neglected to check on him.

Dale appeared to be sleeping when she opened the door, but when she walked over to the bed, he opened his eyes. Even though weak and pale, he managed a smile.

"Good of you ... to come and ... see me."

"How are you feeling today?

"Not too good."

He closed his eyes for several minutes. Deciding he had drifted off to sleep, Marilyn turned to go, until he spoke again.

"Have you seen him?"

For a split second, Marilyn thought he meant Monty, then realized he wasn't talking about their son. He didn't even know about the shooting. "Jake?"

Dale nodded.

Marilyn walked to the window for fear her expression would give her mixed emotions away.

"No. From what Kay tells me, he doesn't want to see either of us."

"We've got to talk to him. It's been the plan from the beginning, remember. When he returned, we'd tell him what happened."

"It's old news, Dale. It won't change anything."

"No, but it will give us peace of mind ... all of us. Besides, a man has a right to know he has a son."

"How can you be so sure?" Marilyn forced herself to smile. "Besides, who says I don't have peace of mind?"

"You can't fool me, sweetheart. We both know you're still in love with Jake. It's why you wanted a divorce. You couldn't stand to live a lie any longer."

Tears stung Marilyn's eyes. "I'm sorry, Dale. You were a good husband, and I do care about you."

Dale nodded. "I know, but your heart has always been with Jake." He closed his eyes again. "Go see him. Convince him to listen to us. We all need that closure."

Marilyn laid her hand against his cheek. "Why don't you rest now? We'll talk more later."

She stepped out of the room to find Kay waiting across the hall, and she motioned for Kay to follow her.

Kay fell into step beside her. "Any change?"

"Dr. Ashworth says he's better than yesterday." Marilyn took a deep breath. "Dale is begging me to talk to Jake."

The intercom interrupted. "Dr. Ashworth to ICU. Dr. Ashworth to ICU."

Marilyn froze, and the two stared at each other. The women raced for the elevator, then paced when it took forever for the doors to open. When they finally reached the second floor, Marilyn hurried for Monty's room, with Kay close behind. A nurse stopped them at the door, placing both hands on Marilyn's shoulders.

"Let me go in," Marilyn begged. "That could be my son." She tried to push past the nurse, who nodded but stood her ground.

"I understand, but Dr. Ashworth is with him now. You can't go in."

Tears rolled down Marilyn's cheeks, and her voice trembled.

"What's happening? I want to see my son." She covered her mouth with her hand as sobs shook her body.

"Ms. Summers, it won't do him or you any good if you go in right now. Let the doctor do his job. Try to stay calm, and wait for Dr. Ashworth to come out."

Kay led Marilyn away from the door toward the waiting area.

"I'm sure Dr. Ashworth will let you know what's going on as soon as he can. Right now, the most important thing he can do is help Monty."

Marilyn dabbed at her eyes with a tissue. "I want to know my son is okay."

It seemed like hours before the doctor came out to her. Fear gripped her again.

"What is it? What's happening to Monty?"

Dr. Ashworth led her to a chair and sat beside her.

"I'm sorry. Monty has slipped into a coma." He took off his glasses. "I'm not sure of the reason at this point, but his body is working to heal itself. We'll just have to wait and see what happens. We're keeping a close watch on him." He propped his glasses back on his nose and took Marilyn's hand in both of his. "You need to rest. Go home. I'll call you if there's any change."

Marilyn shook her head. "I can't leave. I want to be here in case he wakes up."

Dr. Ashworth nodded. "I understand, but at least stretch out for a while on the sofa."

Marilyn turned to Kay. "Why don't you go on home? I'll be fine."

Kay hugged Marilyn. "Only if you promise to call if you need me."

"I promise."

After Kay left, Marilyn slipped off her shoes and lay down on the sofa, but she couldn't relax. Her mind was numb with grief, but it didn't block out the reality of Monty's current state. Thoughts tumbled over each other, begging to be considered and handled. She felt helpless.

God, you're my only hope. You know Monty's need, and you know my heart. I would give every drop of blood I have to save my son's life. I know in times past you visited the sins of the fathers upon their children, but please show mercy to us now. Please, God, forgive Jake and me, and let my son live. And please—please don't let me falter in what I need to do now.

Marilyn slipped her feet into her shoes. She couldn't stand by and let her son die. No matter what the outcome, no matter how he treated her, she had to talk to Jake.

CHAPTER 15

THURSDAY, JUNE 17TH, 10:00 A.M.

Jake sat on the sofa reading the *Archer Springs Weekly News*, his bare feet propped on the coffee table, the door open to let in a breeze. Now that he had electricity, he couldn't wait to get an air conditioner installed.

The paper contained a lot of local small talk. *Brown buys new tractor. The Brewster family hold reunion. Mabel Hunt visits out-of-town friends.* Nothing in the paper hinted at the misery James Sheridan inflicted daily on the town.

A knock at the door interrupted his reading. As he approached the screen door, shock coursed through his body.

Marilyn.

"Hello, Jake."

Every nerve in his system tingled at the sound of her voice.

"I know you don't want to see me, but I—I have to talk to you." She bit her lip and looked away from him.

Jake stood silent, still too surprised to speak.

"Jake, we need to—I mean—" She closed her eyes for a moment then tried again. "Can I come in?"

After another moment of staring, Jake remembered how to breathe. Her visit had caught him as off-guard as a snowstorm in August. He wasn't reacting the way he had imagined he would. The wall of anger he had constructed through the years didn't seem as strong now that the lady stood in front of him.

You're making a mistake if you let her in. Don't allow yourself to be fooled by her again.

"Jake, I'm not here about us, or what happened in the past. I'm here about Monty. I wouldn't bother you if it wasn't important. This is a matter of life and death."

Jake took a deep breath and pushed open the door. If she brought up the past, he would ask her to leave. He could feel her warmth as she brushed past him, and he willed himself to remain calm as her perfume's fragrance filled the room.

Dark circles of pain formed half-moons beneath her lovely hazel eyes, and exhaustion enveloped her like a shroud. In spite of it all, she was still gorgeous. His heart rate spiked off the charts. Then the small nagging voice in his head reminded him—this was the woman who'd betrayed him. He had to keep his head on straight.

"What is it you want to talk about?"

Marilyn inhaled a deep, ragged breath that made her shudder.

"I don't know where to begin." She hesitated a moment, then continued. "I can't thank you enough for saving Monty's life."

Jake shrugged. "Anybody else would have done the same thing." He tried to sound noncommittal, but his voice cracked as though he were thirteen again. His stomach continued to do somersaults, and his heart kept up a steady trot inside his chest.

How could she still have this effect on him after all this time?

"I'm grateful for your help." Marilyn brushed at a loose lock of hair on her forehead with trembling fingers. "I know I'm the last person on earth you want to see, so I'll come straight to the point." She hesitated, and an uncomfortable silence filled the space between them.

Jake couldn't focus. His mind refused to cooperate. He wanted to hold on to his anger, but the sight of her kept pushing it away. She was beautiful and didn't look as though she had aged at all, in spite of the fatigue evident on her face. From the silky brown hair brushing her shoulders to the manicured nails and designer slacks, she was still as stunning as ever.

"I don't know if you've heard. Monty needs a transfusion."

Jake blinked to clear his thoughts. "Yes, Kay mentioned he needs blood. Something about a rare type."

Marilyn nodded, and a single tear slipped down her cheek.

His heart rate picked up. He felt uncomfortable with her eyes searching his face—almost as if she knew he had the kind of blood Monty needed.

"Jake, I remember when your grandfather had that terrible accident. He had a rare blood type, too. You were the only one in the family who had the same type, and you gave blood for him."

Of course. He hadn't thought about his grandfather's wreck in years.

"Jake, my son is dying." Tears glistened on her face.

He forced his emotions to pull away from her. He couldn't allow himself to become involved any deeper.

"I'm sorry about your son. And you're right about the accident. I did give my grandfather blood." Jake ran his hands through his hair. "I don't see how I can help you."

Marilyn brushed at the tears on her face. "Jake, if I have to beg, I will.

Jake stared at her silently, trying to gather his thoughts.

Marilyn took a deep, shuddering breath. "There's something you don't know. I hadn't planned on telling you this ..."

She swallowed hard, and Jake realized she was struggling to speak. She opened her mouth slightly, closed it, looked away, and then faced him. "Please—please, you've got to help Monty."

"Why?"

"Because he's your son."

CHAPTER 16

Jake pulled the truck into the hospital parking lot and parked under the shade of a large cottonwood. He got out and leaned against the tree, its leaves unmoving in the sultry air, trying to collect his thoughts. She'd told him Monty was his son, and then left without another word. She was gone before he could open his mouth, before he could ask all the questions that had haunted him for years. He didn't even know if he believed her.

You're crazy, Reynolds. You're going to give blood to someone who had plans to toss a Molotov cocktail onto your front porch a few days ago. Jake reached for the door handle. *Time to leave. This is a bad idea.*

He stopped. He couldn't silence the internal debate. What if Marilyn was telling him the truth?

If he's my son, I don't want him to die.

Jake climbed the steps leading to the front entrance of the hospital. Cool air swept over him as he entered the building. The gray-haired woman behind the reception desk looked up and smiled.

"May I help you?"

Jake glanced around to see how many other people were within earshot. He wasn't anxious to have anyone else know his intentions, just in case Marilyn was making a fool of him all over again. He lowered his voice.

"I understand you need some AB negative blood for one of your patients."

"Yes, we do."

Jake exhaled the breath he'd been holding. "I'm AB negative."

Relief washed over the woman's face. "Wonderful! You're an answer to prayer."

That was a first. He'd never been told he was the answer to anybody's prayer. "Where do I donate?"

"Right here." She searched for a form in a drawer. "We don't have a blood center in Archer Springs, and we haven't received our delivery from Amarillo yet." She shook her head. "One of the disadvantages of living in a small country town." She held out a clipboard and a ballpoint pen. "Thank you for coming in. If you'll fill out this form, sir, I'll let the lab know you're here."

Jake took the form and pen. He hadn't stopped to think he would have to give his name. "This is all confidential, right?"

"Yes, sir."

He completed the form and waited for the nurse to return. In a few minutes, she was back. She glanced at the form, then nodded at him. "If you'll come with me, Mr. Reynolds, we'll get started."

He followed her down the hall and into a room where a lab technician was setting up the necessary equipment.

Jake closed his eyes and tried to relax. He wasn't afraid of the procedure. The only thing that scared him was having Marilyn or Dale find out he'd done this. He didn't want them thinking they were off the hook, but his mind kept up a running argument.

You're doing the right thing, Reynolds. It's the most honorable thing you've ever done. Forget about who it is, and remember you're saving another human life. Maybe the life of your son. If it were me, I'd want someone to give me blood.

In the cool quiet of the room, with his blood flowing into a bag destined for Marilyn's son, Jake dozed off. The next thing he knew, the technician was pulling the needle from his arm and putting pressure on the puncture site. After a minute, he directed Jake to hold pressure on the spot with his other hand, and Jake obediently pressed down on the gauze while the technician pulled a container of orange juice from a nearby fridge.

"We're all finished, Mr. Reynolds. Drink this, and then you can go as soon as you feel like standing and walking."

Jake sipped the juice, trying to clear the fog from his mind. He glanced at his watch. He had only been here for half an hour, but his sleep-deprived body had gone into rest mode and didn't want to wake up.

The technician, working with the unit of blood and the extra tubes of blood collected along with the bag, glanced at Jake over the top of his glasses.

"Would you like more juice?"

Jake nodded. "If you don't mind. I'm not looking forward to going out into that heat again." After the second container of orange juice, he checked with the technician, who released him. He headed for home, feeling a little better for having done what to him was the right thing.

As he pulled into the driveway, a squad car stopped in front of the house. Jake groaned. He wasn't in the mood for trouble. He met Billy and another deputy in the middle of the yard.

"Hello, Jake."

"What brings you out here?" Jake asked.

Billy tilted his head in the other deputy's direction. "This is Sam Harris."

Jake nodded at the broad-chested, middle-aged deputy standing behind Billy. Harris didn't speak. His arrogant expression caused the muscles in Jake's neck to tighten. He looked away from the deputy and back at Billy.

"Sorry to do this to you." Billy held up a folded piece of paper. "We have a search warrant."

Jake stiffened. "What for? I haven't done anything."

Harris's lip twisted into a sneer. "We're checking all leads."

Jake forced himself to remain calm. "What lead? Someone accusing me of something?"

Billy's eyes pleaded with Jake.

"Come on, Jake, don't make this harder than it is."

Jake unlocked the door and they followed him inside.

"There's not much to see. This is temporary until I decide what to do with the house." He crossed his arms over his chest and stood in the center of the living room, angry underneath his calm exterior, unwilling to sit down while they searched his home.

The officers pulled furniture away from walls, opened drawers, and poked their heads in closets, finding nothing that interested them. As they came down the hall from the bedroom, Sam Harris stopped and looked at the dangling attic rope. He pulled it, and the stairs dropped out of the ceiling. Sam climbed up and disappeared inside the attic.

"What brought this on?" Jake clamped his teeth together to control his temper.

Billy moved into the kitchen, motioned for Jake to follow, and lowered his voice.

"When I arrived at work this morning Sam told me an anonymous call had come in last night after I left the office. The caller wouldn't give his name, but he suggested you might have something to do with Monty's shooting. I told Sam I'd already questioned you, but he wanted to get a court order to search your place."

"Is he one of Sheridan's people?"

Billy nodded and put his finger to his lips.

"Hey," Harris called from the attic doorway, "come and get this box."

Billy climbed the steps to the attic opening and took Aunt Nora's treasure chest from Sam.

Jake held his arms at his sides in an effort not to reach for the box.

"That belonged to my aunt. There's nothing in it but old keepsakes."

Billy set the box on the floor and sorted through the contents. Satisfied it held nothing but photographs and mementos, he scooted it against the end of the sofa and walked back to the attic.

"Hey, Sam. There's nothing here. Let's go."

Harris climbed out of the attic and pushed the stairs back into place. He sneered at Jake again and followed Billy out.

Jake stood on the porch and watched them pull away from the curb. Then he reached into his jeans pocket for his car keys. Time to pay Sheridan another visit.

James Sheridan was in the outer office talking to his secretary when Jake stepped through the door.

"Come in, Mr. Reynolds." Sheridan extended his hand toward Jake, but Jake ignored it, and Sheridan let it drop. "What can I do for you today?"

"Let's talk."

"All right." Sheridan led the way into his office and indicated a wingback chair in front of the desk.

Jake remained standing and glared at Sheridan. He wanted to deck him but knew it wouldn't be wise.

Sheridan sat down in an oversized leather chair. "You've decided to sell me your house?" He smiled, and a smug look crossed his face. "I knew you were a smart man."

"Not on your life. I'm here for another reason altogether."

Sheridan rested his elbows on the polished desktop. "And that is?"

"Do you know Monty Summers?" Jake thought he saw a flicker in Sheridan's eyes, but he wasn't sure.

"Yes, I know Monty."

"Does he work for you?"

Sheridan cleared his throat and leaned back in the chair. "He did, but I assume you've heard of his unfortunate accident."

"As a matter of fact, I'm the one who found him," Jake said, "right behind your office. He'd been shot, and he was almost dead when I arrived."

Sheridan's eyes narrowed. "May I inquire what you were doing behind my office?"

"Looking for you."

A smirk oozed across Sheridan's face. "Most *civilized* people use the front door."

Jake clenched his fists and fought to control his anger. "No one answered the front door, so I came around back. That's when I found Summers." He stared at Sheridan for a moment, wondering how far he could push this man without suffering the same consequences as everyone else.

"I don't suppose you know why Monty Summers drove by my house with a Molotov cocktail in his hand." Jake made it a statement, not a question.

"Now what makes you think I would know what Monty does on his own time?"

"You admitted he's your employee."

Sheridan shook his head. "I'm not responsible for his actions outside his job here."

"So you're saying you know nothing about the house fires?"

Sheridan's face flushed red as he pointed at the door.

"Get out of my office, Reynolds. I don't appreciate being interrogated by a man who's not even a citizen of our town. Go back where you came from. You're not wanted around here."

Jake walked out the door without another word, slamming it behind him. When he reached home, he pulled his truck into the driveway and stepped out of the vehicle. The gate squeaked behind him. He looked over his shoulder to see Carl Malone.

Oh no. Here we go again.

The older man ambled up the walk. "Evening, Jake.

"Hello, Mr. Malone."

The old man eased himself down on the middle step. "How's things going?"

Jake sighed. "Not so good at the moment."

"Anything I can help you with?"

Jake shook his head. "Thank you, Mr. Malone, but I don't know that anyone can help me." He sank down on the step beside the other man.

"More trouble with Sheridan, huh?"

"Yeah. Some officers searched my house this morning on a tip from an anonymous caller."

"You're thinking Sheridan had something to do with it?"

Jake slapped at a mosquito buzzing his ear. "I'm positive he did, but I can't prove it."

They sat in silence for a few moments watching the evening shadows creep across the yard as the sun set.

Mr. Malone pushed his straw hat back on his head. "I understand young Summers is in a coma now."

Jake's heart skipped.

"I know this must be awful hard on Miss Marilyn. First her husband—well, her ex-husband—lands in the hospital, and then her son gets hisself shot." Malone pulled a pocketknife from his overalls and started cleaning his fingernails. "I'd say she must be feeling pretty lonesome about now."

"Yeah."

"You don't sound too sympathetic."

Jake got up from the porch step and strolled out into the yard. He stuffed his hands in his pockets and waited for Malone to continue. He wasn't about to encourage this line of conversation.

The older man stood and slipped the knife back in his pocket. "You might be more sympathetic if you knew all the facts."

"What facts would those be?"

"It's not for me to say." The old man hooked his fingers through the straps of his overalls and continued to stare at Jake.

Jake reached inside his shirt collar and rubbed the back of his hot, sticky neck.

"Look, if you have something to say, say it. I can take it." He kicked at a rock lying in the grass. His daddy had always told him to respect his elders, but Malone was trying his patience big time.

Malone shook his head. "Son, let me give you a piece of advice."

Frustration crawled all over Jake. He raked his hand through his hair. "Do I have a choice?"

"Before you judge people, check out *all* the facts. Walk a mile in their shoes, as the old saying goes." The old man tipped his hat in Jake's direction, then started down the sidewalk. At the gate, he turned around.

"Jake, I'd like to see you get the past straightened out before you leave town."

Jake kicked the rock again, harder.

"I'm not accountable to anyone in this town." As soon as the words left his lips, shame swept over him. Malone was an old man who thought he could help change twenty-five years of pain.

Without another word, Malone pushed open the gate and ambled down the street.

CHAPTER 17

FRIDAY, JUNE 18TH, 11:00 A.M.

Mr. Woods looked up from his television program when Jake entered the lobby. "Jake, my boy, it's good to see you."

Jake shook the old man's hand. "How are you doing?"

"Aw, I can't complain. It's nothing but old age anyway." He pointed at a brown leather chair. "Sit in that chair over by the window fan. It's already hotter than blue blazes out there today. Too hot for fishing, I can tell you that. Can I get you a glass of iced tea? Kay made a big pitcher for me last night before she went home."

Jake sank into the chair, allowing the fan to hit him full in the face. "That sounds good."

Mr. Woods disappeared for a few moments, then returned with two glasses of iced tea.

"By the way, Jake, the postman brought mail for you yesterday." Mr. Woods tottered over to the desk and shuffled through some papers until he found what he was looking for. He handed Jake an envelope from Masters Manufacturing.

Jake tore it open and glanced inside. A check for ten thousand dollars. Severance pay. He swallowed hard. It was a little frightening to lose a job you'd had all your adult life and hold what was left in the palm of your hand.

Mr. Woods sat in the chair next to Jake. "Good news, I hope."

"It's from my old boss." He folded the envelope and stuck it in his shirt pocket. "He sent my severance pay, which I can sure use. I've spent most of my cash fixing up Aunt Nora's house."

Mr. Woods took a long sip.

"Ahhh, nothing better than a glass of iced tea on a hot day." He wiped his mouth with the back of his hand. "How come you don't call it your house? It is, you know."

Jake laughed. "Somehow, I can't get used to that fact, and Sheridan certainly doesn't want me to."

Mr. Woods shook his head. "Have you made any headway with him?"

"No. I was there yesterday, and he threw me out of his office for asking him about the house fires."

"He doesn't like it when people cross him. I'd be on my guard if I were you."

Jake sighed, exasperation building inside again.

"What would you do if someone called the police station and implicated you in a shooting?"

Mr. Woods frowned, deep lines creasing his brow. "Do they think you had something to do with Monty's shooting?"

"Somebody is trying to pin something on me, and my guess is it's Sheridan. It's another scare tactic because I won't sell him the house. If I phoned him right now and offered to sell it to him, he'd call off his hounds."

"I admire you for standing your ground, but be careful." Mr. Woods finished his tea and set the glass on the floor next to his chair. "By the way, have you heard how Monty and Dale are doing today?"

Jake shook his head. "I don't think there's been any change."

"Kay's been mighty worried about Dale and his son. She won't eat, doesn't get much sleep, still tries to work here some every day. I told her I could handle this place fine until things change, but she won't listen."

They fell silent for a few minutes, the whir of the fan the only sound in the room.

Mr. Woods cleared his throat. "Have you given much thought to our last conversation?"

"Concerning?"

"Your intentions regarding Kay."

Jake rested his sweating tea glass on his knee.

"We haven't spent any time together the last few days. Kay has other things on her mind." He remembered their conversation a few days earlier regarding her feelings about Dale.

"Are you saying you're not going to pursue the relationship?"

Jake shook his head. "We're friends, Mr. Woods. Ask Kay. She'll tell you. There's nothing between us but friendship."

The old man winked. "I was hoping the two of you might get involved a little deeper."

"I think we're as involved as we're going to get." Jake watched the circle of dampness grow larger on his knee as the sweat ran down the glass and soaked into his jeans.

"Cupid's lost his touch, huh?"

Jake laughed. "He lost it a long time ago where I'm concerned."

"I don't believe that for one minute. When the right woman comes along, that arrow will head straight for your heart."

Jake didn't respond. That arrow had made its way into his heart years ago and had been lodged there ever since. He'd felt its stabbing force too many times over the last twenty-five years not to recognize the feeling if it came again. He stood.

"I need to get going. I have an air conditioner to install."

FRIDAY, JUNE 18TH, 1:00 P.M.

Marilyn glanced up from her newspaper to see Dr. Ashworth enter the waiting room, a big smile on his face.

"I have some good news for you."

She tossed the paper on the table and stood. "Did Monty wake up?"

"No, he isn't awake, but we did have an AB negative blood donor come in."

Marilyn closed her eyes and let out a sigh of relief. "Thank God, my son's going to live." She opened her eyes. "He is, isn't he?"

"It will be a while before we know anything, but he has a good chance now that he's receiving blood. Hang in there, Marilyn. Things are looking up."

"What's looking up?" Kay asked as she came in.

"Someone donated blood for Monty."

Kay grabbed Marilyn and hugged her. "That's wonderful."

Dr. Ashworth patted Marilyn's shoulder. "Monty has been through a lot. Don't expect miracles too soon."

Jake watched the young deputy get out of the Mustang and make his way up the walk. Billy wasn't in uniform. Jake stepped to the door and pushed open the screen.

"Getting to be a regular visitor around here, aren't you?"

Billy grinned. "Relax. It's not business this time."

"I figured as much, since you're wearing jeans and driving a Mustang."

Billy stuffed his hands in his pockets and squinted in the late evening sun. "Came by to see how you're doing."

"Making house calls now?"

Billy laughed and rocked back on the heels of his boots. "Only for special people."

Jake stepped out onto the porch. "What makes me so special?"

"Anyone who can face down trouble like you do rates high in my book."

"Speaking of trouble, did they ever find who shot Monty Summers?"

Billy shook his head. "We all know who did it, but he won't be arrested. He knows too much about this town and the people."

Jake nodded in the direction of the door. "Come on inside where it's cool. I'm gonna have a bologna sandwich. Want one?"

"Sounds good to me." Billy followed Jake inside and sat down at the kitchen table.

Jake set bread, meat, and cheese on the table, then fished inside the ice chest for mayo and drinks. "Sorry it's not steak and salad. A fridge is the next thing on my list."

Billy helped himself to the bread. "Hey, I was raised on bologna sandwiches."

"Same here." Jake popped the top on a drink and took a big swig. He watched Billy make a Dagwood-sized sandwich. "What will happen to Sheridan if Monty dies?"

Billy picked up the sandwich, ready to take a bite. He stopped mid-way to his mouth. "I don't even want to think about that."

Jake spread mayo on two slices of bread and reached for the meat. "Are you saying he'll still be free, even after committing murder?"

"Let's say I don't know of anyone in this town who would show up on his doorstep with a warrant." Billy took another bite. "Unless you're willing to pin on a badge."

Jake leaned back in his chair and laughed. "Not only would I be unwilling, but I'm sure there's not anyone who would offer me the opportunity." He watched Billy eat and shook his head. "Didn't your mother ever tell you it's bad manners to talk with your mouth full?"

Billy grinned. "She said it's okay as long as we're here in Archer Springs. It's when we leave town and go to the city that I have to be on my best behavior."

Jake washed his sandwich down with some soda. "So, you were raised in Archer Springs?"

Billy nodded. "Delivered right here in Archer Springs General by Dr. Ashworth on May 10, 1958." He laid down his sandwich and reached for his drink. "My folks are gone, though. I lost both of them within a year of each other seven years ago, right after I graduated from high school."

"Any brothers or sisters?"

"I have an older brother living in Austin. We get together now and then. And Aunt Rose lives in the nursing home on the edge of town. I've got cousins scattered around the country, but we're not close. Haven't seen them since I was a kid. What about you?"

"My situation isn't any better." Jake stood and gathered the meat and cheese and carried it to the ice chest. "Let's finish off this gourmet meal with some oatmeal cookies. Unless you're in a hurry ...?"

Billy wiped his mouth with the paper towel Jake offered. "I never turn down oatmeal cookies. They're my favorite." He bit into a cookie. "Did you come back to Archer Springs to repair the house?"

"Yeah. I would've never come back if Sheridan hadn't written me that letter." Jake reached inside the bag for another cookie. "Ever think about leaving here?"

Billy shook his head. "Nah. I like it here, 'n I like my job. I know everyone in town. That's a pretty comfortable feeling. Know what I mean?"

"If you think it's comfortable now, you should've been here twenty-five years ago. It was paradise. If people don't wake up, Sheridan's going to destroy this place, along with that feeling."

They finished off the bag of cookies and silence dropped over them again.

Jake glanced over at the younger man. It had been a long time since he'd felt this kind of camaraderie with someone, and he didn't even know Billy that well.

Billy glanced at him. "How long you planning to stay?"

Jake shifted his position and stretched his legs. "A few more days. Why?"

"I'll be sorry to see you go. You're about the only person I can talk to other than Mr. Woods."

Jake didn't respond. Yesterday he would have said he couldn't wait to leave, but today ... he didn't know.

CHAPTER 18

SATURDAY, JUNE 19TH, 2:00 P.M.

Kay stood at the door to Dale's hospital room and breathed a prayer of thanks. She knocked and waited.

"Come in." Dale sat on the edge of the bed reading a newspaper.

"Look at you. This is wonderful."

Dale smiled and laid his newspaper to one side. "I think I'm going to make it."

Kay pulled a chair next to the bed and sat down. "Of course you will. This town couldn't operate without you."

Dale's smile faded. "You know, I've been doing a lot of thinking, lying here day after day. I don't like what's happening to Archer Springs. Sheridan has changed our town, and not for the better."

Kay frowned. "But I thought you liked his ideas." She cleared her throat and started over. "I mean, you were one of his staunchest supporters at one time."

"I know, but he's not the person I believed him to be. The night of my heart attack, I went to see Sheridan. I didn't know he was going to start burning real estate." Dale poured some ice water into the glass by his bed and took a sip. "It was okay to demolish those two abandoned houses at the edge of town. But he started forcing people out of their homes. I told him I couldn't go along with that."

Kay's breath caught in her throat. "What did he say? Did he threaten you?"

"He laughed and told me not to get in his way, or I'd be next. I made up my mind right then that something needed to be done. But by the time I got home that night, my chest hurt so bad I knew I was in trouble. If Monty hadn't found me when he did, I wouldn't be alive." He set the glass back on the table. "I've got to do something before Sheridan destroys Archer Springs."

Kay leaned over and touched his arm. "You concentrate on getting better right now. That's the important thing."

Dale smiled and reached for her hand.

"You've been a lifesaver, coming to visit every day, taking my messages to Jake." He frowned. "I've missed Monty, though. Wonder what's keeping that boy so occupied he can't even visit his old man in the hospital?"

Kay's heart skipped a beat. She searched for an excuse. "You know how this younger generation is. They get wrapped up in their own lives." She held her breath, hoping Dale would accept her explanation.

Dale cocked his head to one side and watched her for a moment, then shrugged.

"If you say so. I guess we were the same when we were kids." He took another sip of water and changed the subject. "Jake's bitter, isn't he?"

Kay nodded. "Yes."

Dale ran his hand through his hair. "I can't blame him. That was a pretty brutal blow we dealt him. I hoped that after all these years, he would let bygones be bygones. Guess the old cliché about time healing all wounds doesn't apply in this case."

"I've tried to talk to him about it, but he won't budge."

"When I get out of here, I plan to go see him myself. I've carried this guilt around long enough."

"You still feel guilty after all this time?"

Dale sighed. "You have no idea what it's been like all these years. Living with the knowledge I hurt someone I loved like a brother. It's been a heavy load to carry." He shook his head. "Not only hurt him, but changed his whole life. I don't think a day has gone by when I haven't thought about Jake in one way or another and wondered if he was okay."

"I know you and Marilyn made a mistake ..." Kay hesitated and played with the bangles on her right arm, sliding them up and down. She glanced at Dale again. He was watching her, his blue eyes never leaving her face. "I mean ..." Kay stopped and looked out the window. "If you were that much in love, why couldn't the two of you have told Jake and me before he left that summer?"

Sadness filled Dale's eyes, causing Kay to regret her prying, insensitive words. He looked down at his hands for a moment. When he looked up again, Kay thought he had somehow aged in those brief seconds.

"Sometimes life hands out hard choices. That's what happened with Marilyn and me. We didn't plan it this way. We were two kids who thought we had everything figured out. Then life threw us a curve ball."

"A curve ball?"

Dale shook his head. "There are things you don't know, Kay. Things nobody in this town knows. Trust me when I say Marilyn and I did the only thing we knew to do under the circumstances."

"Maybe so, but we're talking about people's lives here. Jake was in love with Marilyn. The two of you destroyed his future. I don't think life has been the same for him since then." Kay blinked against the tears forming in her eyes.

Dale sighed. "You can't say anything to me I haven't said to myself over and over. Sometimes you have to be willing to sacrifice one life for another."

A stream of anger trickled over her. "You're saying what the two of you wanted was more important than hurting Jake, is that it? His feelings weren't important?"

Dale frowned. When he spoke, his voice seemed embedded with steel.

"I'm sorry, but this conversation is over." He stood and walked to the window, his back to her. "I won't tell you any more than what I've already said. Don't ever ask me about this again."

Kay was speechless. She felt like a small child who'd been reprimanded. Hot tears stung her eyes and her face burned with embarrassment, but she respected Dale's feelings. Whatever had happened between him and Marilyn was a private matter. She picked up her purse and stepped over to Dale. She laid her hand on his shoulder.

"I'm sorry. I shouldn't have pried into your personal affairs."

She waited for Dale to respond. When he didn't, she turned and walked out of the room.

SUNDAY, JUNE 20TH, 3:00 A.M.

Jake startled awake, his senses alert. He lay still, waiting, listening for some sound, an intruder maybe, but he heard nothing. He sat up on the edge of the bed, trying to keep the old springs from squeaking. Every nerve in his body whispered that something was wrong. Then he smelled smoke.

He jumped to his feet and hurried to the doorway. He heard the fire hissing before he ever saw it. By the time he reached the kitchen, flames were licking at the curtains Kay had hung for him. Smoke burned his eyes. He ran back to the bedroom and grabbed the clothes hanging on the bedpost. He felt for his boots, and ran into the living room, stumbling against Aunt Nora's treasure chest jamming his toes. *Blast it, Billy. Why'd you leave it sitting here?*

The pain paralyzed him for a second. Then he grabbed the chest and headed outside. Jake was glad for the darkness as he stepped out on the porch half-naked. He set the chest down and pulled on his jeans and boots and grabbed the chest up again.

A siren wailed in the distance. Someone had already called the fire department. Jake glanced around for some place to set the chest and saw the pickup—far too close to the house. Jake reached in his pocket for the keys. He threw the chest on the front seat and hurriedly backed out of the driveway. With the truck out of danger, he ran back toward the house, denial screaming through his mind.

The fire truck rolled to a stop, red lights flashing, siren blaring. The firemen launched themselves from the vehicle and unrolled the hoses, spraying multiple streams of water into the flames. The fire continued wrapping its hungry tongues around the house, while Jake stood at the edge of the yard, watching the last monument to his family go up in smoke.

People arrived out of nowhere, milling around on the street. Some had gathered in a little group next door, talking low. Jake viewed the scene as if in a trance. It felt as though a huge movie screen had been erected on Orchard Street, and he had a front row seat for the show. Only this horror script was real.

After what seemed like hours, a fireman approached him. "I'm sorry, sir. We can't save it. These older homes go up like fireworks on the Fourth of July." He shook his head. "You're mighty lucky you got out alive."

Jake nodded, numb with disbelief. The fireman went back to his truck where the men had already begun rolling up the hoses. One by one the spectators wandered back to their own homes. The fire truck finally roared to life, and he raised his head to see it pulling away, leaving him alone on the street. He surveyed the devastation around him. Nothing left but a pile of smoking, charred wood. Jake sat on the curb and covered his face with his hands.

I'm sorry, Aunt Nora. I tried to save the house. This is Sheridan's doing. I'll get that guy and make him pay, if it's the last thing I do.

Jake trudged to his truck beaten and drained. He climbed inside and leaned his head back against the seat. His reason for being here had just been eliminated, the last tie to his past gone. He gripped the steering wheel and bit his lip to keep the tears at bay, but they streamed down his face anyway, mixing with the blood on his lip. He remembered something his dad had said to him when he was twelve, something like, "Men don't cry. They never let their feelings show."

Well, Dad, this time you were wrong. He leaned his forehead against the steering wheel. *I always seem to lose everything I thought was mine.*

CHAPTER 19

Sunday, June 20th, 8:00 a.m.

Jake awoke to early morning sunlight streaming through the truck window. At first, he couldn't focus. Then he remembered the fire. The blackened shell of the house still smoldered.

His head ached, and his muscles demanded to be stretched out of their cramped position. His clothes clung to his damp, sweaty body. He smelled like smoke. He climbed out and walked across the street to where the house had stood, and grief crept over him as last night's scene replayed in his mind.

The iron bed still stood in the spot where he'd been asleep when the fire broke out. The mattress had been reduced to a soggy lump of scorched fabric. The sofa stood like a skeleton, baring its bones to the sun. He kicked a half-burned piece of lumber out of the way to find a blackened coffee mug underneath.

Anger swept over Jake as he surveyed what remained of his inheritance. The promise he'd made to Aunt Nora lay cremated, all because of some greedy no-good who thought he could rule the town.

He strode back to his truck and jumped in. The engine roared to life. He jammed the accelerator and made the tires smoke and squeal. He knew it wouldn't do any good to report the fire, but it would look suspicious on his part if he didn't at least tell someone in authority. Even as he headed into town, he was sure they already knew the big old house on Orchard Street had been reduced to ashes.

Billy met him at the door and motioned for Jake to step back outside.

"I heard what happened. I'm sorry, Jake." He scratched his head, then smoothed his hair in place. "One thing for sure, it couldn't have been Monty, seeing as how he's still in the hospital. Funny thing though, the suspect was driving Monty's white Volkswagen."

"Who do you think it was?"

Billy shook his head. "Seems one of your neighbors had insomnia last night. His air conditioner wasn't working, and he was sleeping on a cot on the front porch." Billy pulled a piece of paper out of his shirt pocket and glanced at it. "Name's Simmons. You know him?"

Jake frowned. "I haven't met any of the neighbors."

Billy stuffed the paper back in his pocket. "Simmons says the Volkswagen circled the block before it stopped across the street from your place. The driver got out of the car and sneaked around to the rear of the house. He was acting so suspicious, Mr. Simmons got up and watched. A few minutes later, the driver came back to his car and left. Simmons noticed flames and called the fire department."

"What are the chances there are two white Volkswagens in this town?"

"A million to one," Billy said, "but Simmons caught a glimpse of part of the license plate. The driver wasn't too smart. He parked under a streetlight. The numbers match Monty's VW."

"Where do we go from here?"

"We're looking for the driver, but we don't have much to go on. The car was sitting in the driveway at the Summers home this morning. That's where we parked it the night Monty was shot. It's being checked for prints. Fresh tracks in the driveway indicated the car had been moved."

"Let me know what you find out." He looked down at himself. "I've got to get out of these stinky clothes."

Billy wrinkled his nose and frowned. "I wondered where that smell was coming from." He grinned.

Jake wiggled a finger at him. "Watch yourself. I'm not in the mood for jokes." He started to walk away, then turned back and offered his hand. "Thanks for what you're trying to do. I know it isn't easy under the circumstances."

Billy nodded. "Wish I could do more."

SUNDAY, JUNE 20TH, 9:00 A.M.

Mr. Woods's snoring penetrated the quiet motel lobby. Jake hated waking the old man, but he needed a bath. He smelled like smoke and stale body odor. He was anxious to get some soap and water on his skin. The floor creaked as Jake walked toward the desk.

Mr. Woods opened his eyes.

"Oh, Jake, it's you. Thank goodness you're okay."

Jake nodded and yawned. "I'm fine, Mr. Woods, sleepy and tired. I suppose you heard about the fire."

"Yes." He shook his head. "I'm sorry you had to become one of Sheridan's victims."

"Not half as much as I am." Jake leaned against the counter. "Looks like I'm going to have to move back in here for a while."

"Glad to have you, son. I've missed having you around." Mr. Woods selected a key from the wall. "Your old room is empty."

Jake filled the clawfoot tub with hot water and stepped in. He reached for the bar of Dial soap, slid down into the tub up to his neck, and closed his eyes. Someone or something had it in for him.

I've got to get out of here. Why am I staying here putting myself through this misery? The only good thing to come out of this is that I might have a son, if Marilyn's telling me the truth. But I still have one last thing to do ... get rid of Sheridan.

After his bath, Jake dressed in the same reeking clothes and went out to shop for necessities, grateful he had opened an account at the bank and stashed some cash in the glove compartment of the truck. Otherwise it would have been lost in the fire.

When he returned to the motel, his arms loaded with packages, Kay was sitting in the lobby talking with Mr. Woods. She rushed to Jake and threw her arms around him, packages and all.

"I'm so sorry about the fire." She released him and stepped away. "Why didn't you call me?"

"No time. Everything happened too fast."

"What are you going to do now?"

Jake shrugged. "The house is gone. Sheridan got his way." He rubbed his eyes. "One thing's for certain, though. I'm going to make sure he gets what's coming to him."

SUNDAY, JUNE 20TH, 10:00 P.M.

Jake slipped out the front door of the motel. Instead of walking across the deserted square, he followed the sidewalk around, careful to stay in the shadows.

At Sheridan's place, he slowed his pace but kept moving in case someone was watching. He glanced in the window as he walked by. A light shone beneath the door to the room he knew was the office.

The sound of a car engine came closer. Jake stepped around the edge of the building and flattened himself against it. A patrol car eased by, but the officer didn't look his way. Jake breathed a sigh of relief and made his way around to the alley. As he reached Sheridan's back door, voices drifted out into the summer air. He contemplated busting through the door, but decided doing so might get him shot.

A silvery moon bathed the alley in light. Jake moved into the shadow of the building near a window. The voices grew louder. He recognized Sheridan's voice. The other one sounded like a woman.

"I've been good to you, James," the female voice said. "I've sneaked around meeting you at all hours of the night in sleazy motels. I've done your dirty work. I thought we had something special. Don't try to weasel out on me now."

"It's been fun, but it's over. I won't be needing your services any longer."

Jake heard the contempt in Sheridan's voice. He wished he could peek into the window without being seen, but he couldn't risk it.

The woman's voice rose, a hint of hysteria evident.

"My services? Is that what you think of me, that I've been servicing you all these months like a common prostitute? I thought I meant something to you."

Jake moved closer to the window, but Sheridan and his visitor were out of view. *Better to wait until the woman leaves to confront Sheridan.*

"Have I ever promised you anything other than a paycheck?"

Sheridan seemed to be taunting her. Hadn't he ever heard the saying, *Hell hath no fury like a woman scorned*? Sheridan might be getting his due from someone else first, someone with a bigger axe to grind than his own.

"You're a liar and a cheat, James. I never figured you for that kind of man."

Sheridan laughed. "Well, it gets me what I want, and what I want right now is for you to get out of my face."

"And this is going to get me what *I* want."

Jake heard the tone of her voice change from complaint to threat.

"Okay, put the gun away." Sheridan's voice had taken on a more serious note. "You'll hurt somebody."

"I want something for all these months of servicing you, as you call it. I want some of the money you've been taking from the people in this town."

"You've been paid for every job you've done and you know it."

"I'm warning you. I can use this thing if I have to. Now that I know what you are, it won't bother me one bit to blow away that fake smile."

Sheridan laughed. "You're not in any position to talk about the kind of person I am. You've got a rap sheet a mile long."

"You don't know anything about me. Quit trying to call my bluff."

"I know you've spent time behind bars. Hmm. Let me see now. There was the drunk and disorderly charge a few years back. And I believe you were arrested for theft in Austin last year. Add to that illegal possession of drugs, and the hit-and-run accident you managed to wiggle out of." Sheridan laughed again. "Sweetheart, you're not a good candidate for Miss Wholesome."

"You think that's going to stop me from pulling the trigger?"

"You won't get away with it."

"And who's going to stop me? Not you. You won't be around to say anything."

"Give me the gun."

"I'm warning you. Stay where you are."

The sounds of a scuffle came from inside. Jake leaned closer to the window trying to see in. A gunshot reverberated through the darkness, and he ducked.

The door flew open and a woman ran out, gun in hand. In the light from the doorway Jake caught a glimpse of a ponytail blowing behind her as she disappeared down the alley. Jake ran to the door.

Sheridan lay crumpled on the floor, blood soaking the front of his shirt. His eyes—surprise evident in them—stared at Jake. His mouth hung partway open, as though he had been talking when the bullet found its mark. His breathing came in short gasps. He groaned and tried to lift his hand toward Jake. For a split second, Jake thought of walking away and leaving him there. Someone else had gotten rid of his enemy for him. Who would care?

If he waited long enough, it would be too late. Then Aunt Nora's voice sliced through his thoughts.

For if ye forgive men their trespasses, your heavenly Father will also forgive you.

Jake stepped over the body and picked up the phone.

CHAPTER 20

MONDAY, JUNE 21ST, 1:00 A.M.

"How do you always manage to turn up at crime scenes?" Billy jotted notes on his clipboard as he talked.

"Lucky, I guess." Jake shook his head. "Maybe the real question is why all the crime scenes are at Sheridan's office."

Billy took off his Stetson and laid it on the desk. "This time the sheriff himself is going to question you, and he won't be as easy on you as I am." He sat down behind the desk and leaned back.

Jake sighed and rubbed his eyes.

"I told you. The woman with a ponytail is the one who shot him. She had the gun in her hand when she came running out the door. Find her, and you've got the guilty party." He stretched his legs out in front of him. "Besides, if I was guilty, I wouldn't have reported it, would I?"

Billy shook his head.

"Jake, you know I believe you, but it's not that simple. Abel's gonna want to know what you were doing in Sheridan's office. He doesn't know you like I do."

Jake stood and walked to the window overlooking the town square. The town lay sleeping, unaware their enemy had been transported to the hospital, his life hanging by a thread.

He turned back to Billy. "I wasn't in Sheridan's office. I was standing outside. How long before your boss gets here? I've had a rough twenty-four hours. I need some sleep."

"He'll be here as soon as they get things cleared up at Sheridan's place."

The door opened, and Sheriff Abel Madison lumbered in.

"Billy, is there any coffee made? I need some caffeine." When he spoke, the sound was more like a roar than a human voice.

Jake studied him from across the room. Abel's huge belly jiggled when he walked. The buttons on his uniform shirt looked as though they might pop off at any moment. Billy had told him Abel loved Mexican food and fried catfish. Billy had also told him Abel was a workaholic. Nobody loved his job more than Abel Madison. He spent long hours at the office and had been known to go without sleep many nights in order to serve and protect Archer Springs. In other words, he was a gung-ho sheriff who would like nothing better than to arrest a stranger in town for the shooting.

Madison sat down behind his desk and pulled a cigar out of his pocket. He lit it, then looked in Jake's direction. "Are you the witness?"

"Yes, sir."

"Well, come on over here and let's get down to business." Madison took a big puff on the cigar, and smoke billowed from his Jimmy Durante-like nose.

Jake sat down in the chair in front of Madison's desk and leaned to one side to avoid the cigar smoke. Madison looked at him through bloodshot eyes.

"What I want to know is, what were you doing in Sheridan's office tonight?"

"I wanted to talk to Sheridan. No one was in the front office, so I went around to the back door."

"Then how come you never knocked on the door?"

"I didn't say I never knocked."

"Don't be a smart aleck." Madison blew smoke in Jake's direction. "Sheridan might not be in critical condition right now if you'd done something to distract the killer."

Jake forced himself to remain calm even though he was beginning to feel like the criminal in this situation.

"The truth is, when I walked up to the door, I could hear them arguing. I decided it was best to wait until the woman left before I went in." Jake turned his face away from the choking smoke in search of fresh air.

"Billy, what in tarnation is taking you so long?" Madison yelled. "How long does it take to pour a cup of coffee?" He turned his attention back to Jake. "What can you tell me about the person you saw?"

"Not much. I'm sure it was a woman because of her voice, but I couldn't see her face. When she came out the door, she had a gun." Jake stifled a yawn. "Oh, and she had her hair in a ponytail."

Madison chewed on the stump of his cigar.

"You don't seem to be taking this very serious. There's been an attempted homicide, and you were on the premises. Doesn't that concern you?"

"Yes, sir, it does. No disrespect intended, but I haven't had much sleep. My house burned last night, and I slept in my truck."

Madison frowned. "Oh, yeah. I'd forgotten about that." He blew a smoke ring in Jake's direction. "Sounds like motive to me."

Billy walked over to the desk and set a cup of coffee in front of the sheriff.

"About time." Madison took a big swig and turned back to Jake. "After the woman ran out, what happened?"

"I went inside and found Sheridan lying on the floor with a hole in his chest. He was still breathing. That's when I called 9-1-1."

Madison leaned forward in his chair and took a big draw on the cigar.

"You seem to have a knack for turning up at crime scenes. Why is that?"

Jake sat a little straighter.

"I've not planned it that way. Both times, I've had business with Sheridan. When I arrived, trouble was already brewing. Seems to me Mr. Sheridan has a knack for causing problems." Madison glared at him, and Jake regretted his last comment.

Madison chewed on his cigar and studied the paperwork Billy had given him. "Okay, Reynolds, you can go. Don't leave town until we get this thing settled. I may need you to identify a ponytail."

CHAPTER 21

Jake sat up in bed and glanced at his watch. *Nine o'clock.* He felt as though it had only been a few minutes since he laid down. It had been three a.m. when he'd left the sheriff's office and crept back into the motel.

A knock sounded at the door. "Jake? How about some breakfast?"

"Be there in a minute." Jake grabbed a new pair of jeans and a shirt from the stash he had bought the day before. He pulled them on, splashed water on his face, and combed his hair, then walked across the hall to Mr. Woods's quarters.

"Come on in." Mr. Woods set a plate of biscuits on the table. "I've got some news for you."

"Don't tell me you've already heard about Sheridan." Jake helped himself to a hot biscuit, split it open and spread butter on it.

Mr. Woods stared at Jake. "How do you know about it?"

Jake took a bite before speaking.

"It's a long story, but I'm the one who reported it." He filled Mr. Woods in on the details while they finished off the pan of biscuits and a pot of coffee.

"Well, maybe this will put a stop to some of his shenanigans for a while. No more house fires, at least for a few days." He stopped and looked at Jake. "I'm sorry, Jake. That must be a painful subject for you right now."

He swallowed the last of his coffee and leaned back in his chair.

"I hate that I couldn't keep my promise to Aunt Nora and Uncle George. They meant a lot to me, and I believe in keeping promises."

"You did the best you could." Mr. Woods stood and began clearing the dishes from the table. "Knowing Nora and George Reynolds, I'd say they wouldn't hold it against you."

Jake nodded. "You're right, but I had a lot of good times in that old house when I was a kid."

Mr. Woods squirted dish soap into the sink and turned on the hot water.

"The house may be gone, but you still have the memories. Even a fire can't take those away from you."

After breakfast, Jake left the motel and headed for Orchard Street. It was up to him to clean up the fire damage. When he pulled in front of the house, sadness enveloped him. He stared at the burned remains of his inheritance. Mr. Woods was right. He could keep those memories alive, but it wouldn't be the same. He walked around the burned-out shell, remembering his talks with Aunt Nora, his whittling lessons from Uncle George. He could almost hear their laughter and voices. Tears stung his eyes. He rubbed his hands across his face.

I'm sorry. I tried to keep my promise, but I was too late.

"Stirring up painful memories, are you?"

Carl Malone stood at the edge of the yard. "It's okay to grieve. It's a part of living, but once the grieving is over, you have to go on with life."

Jake tried to swallow the lump in his throat. "Things were so simple then. It's a shame they had to change."

"That's what life is all about, son. Change. Nothin' don't ever stay the same. You have to learn to swim the river, rapids and all."

Jake kicked at a piece of charred wood. "Sometimes I feel as though the river is taking me under."

Mr. Malone picked up a table leg that had survived the fire. "When you can't swim, lie back and float until you regain your strength. The Good Book says, 'We walk by faith, and not by sight.' When you can't see your way clear, keep the faith. God will show up on the scene when it's time." He tossed the table leg into the ash pile. "I'm sorry about your house, but maybe it's for the best."

"What do you mean by that?"

"Sometimes we try to hold onto things we need to let go. In your case, I'd say you've been living in the past for a long time."

Anger rippled through Jake. "What would you know about how I've been living?"

"I know you've been carrying around a grudge against two people who deserve forgiveness. You're acting like the thing happened yesterday."

Jake stared at Malone. He wanted to dispute the man's words, but something about them made sense. Maybe he needed a fresh start. Jake squinted at Malone.

"Tell me something. Have you become a preacher since your retirement from the burger business?"

Malone laughed. "No, I'm not a preacher." He turned to leave. "Remember what I told you about checking out all the facts. Do it, son, before it's too late. You've already started the process by giving blood to young Summers. Keep moving in that general direction."

Jake's heart hammered against his chest.

"How did you know I gave blood?"

"When I heard someone had donated, I figured it to be you. Anyone else in town would have come forward sooner, seeing as how it's one of our own that's in need." He smiled. "You used to be one of us. Could be again, if you'd a mind to."

Jake sighed. "There's nothing here for me. I'll be moving on in a few days." *Unless Monty really is my son. That could change things.*

Mr. Malone pushed his hat back and scratched his head. "Do me a favor before you leave. Check out a few things."

Jake stared at the older man.

"You keep telling me to check things out, but I have no idea where to start."

"Go to the courthouse and look at the birth records in 1958." He held up one finger. "That's all I'm saying for now."

Frustration crept over Jake. "Whose record?"

The old man walked out to the street, then looked back at Jake. "Monty Summers."

Jake stared after Malone, his heart rate accelerating. Maybe the old man knew something. Maybe Marilyn *was* telling the truth, not just using him to save her son. A chill swept over Jake in spite of the summer heat. She wouldn't have come to him without a good reason. It *was* time to check out the facts, and no better time than now. He reached in his pocket for his keys and headed for the truck.

A few minutes later, Jake pushed open the door to the ancient stone courthouse. Once inside, he paused to allow his eyes to adjust to the cool, dark interior. A sign on the wall listed the County Clerk's office as Room 105. An attractive young woman smiled at him.

"May I help you, sir?"

"Yes, I'd like to see the birth records from 1958, please." The girl disappeared. Jake paced back and forth in front of the counter until she returned carrying a large volume.

"Here you go. This volume covers 1950-1959." She laid it on the counter.

Jake stared at the cover of the book, excitement and anxiety shoving against each other inside his chest. Ever since Marilyn had told him Monty was his, he'd tried putting two and two together, and a few minutes ago, Malone had told him to check Monty's birth record. He now felt sure of what he was going to see in this book. For the first time in his life, he felt vulnerable, almost fearful.

"Sir, is something wrong?"

"No, everything's fine." He opened the book, and she returned to her desk. He fanned the pages, his heart thumping as he searched for March 1958. When he found the page, he took a deep breath before he looked at the information. Only one birth had been recorded for that month. Jake's heart pounded and his fingers trembled on the page. *Montcrief Allen Summers, Born: March 15, 1958, Archer Springs, Texas. Father: Jackson Dale Summers, Mother: Marilyn Baker Summers, Blood Type: AB Negative.*

Jake closed the book and walked out of the building, not allowing himself to think until he reached the truck. Marilyn had given the baby his grandfather's name. She wouldn't have done that unless …

He broke out in a cold sweat, and his hands trembled on the steering wheel as the memory of their last night together in 1957 flashed before him. He closed his eyes, trying to wrap his brain around what was becoming clearer to him every second. Marilyn hadn't lied to him. *He was Monty's father.*

This was what Malone had been trying to tell him the past few weeks. *Check things out, Jake. Walk a mile in their shoes.* But how did Malone know? It was time he turned the tables and paid the older man a visit.

Jake drove to the two-story house he remembered from childhood. He felt a little nervous about questioning the man. He sat for a moment, trying to calm himself, scanning the scene before him. A painter stood on a ladder applying fresh paint to a gable. A young boy knelt on his knees and pulled weeds from a flower bed. A simple picture of life. But Jake knew without even talking to Malone that nothing would ever be simple for him again. He climbed out of the truck and started up the walk.

Malone opened the door before Jake even reached the porch.

"Come in out of the heat."

He led the way into a large room filled with antiques and the scent of age. Jake thought Mr. Malone looked a little out of place in his overalls, but it didn't seem to bother the other man.

"Nice house."

Malone nodded. "Thank you. Bertha loved decorating this place. I've kept everything as she left it when she passed five years ago. Someone comes in and cleans it every week." He smiled and lowered himself onto the sofa. "Sit a spell, Jake."

Jake cleared his throat. "I think you know why I'm here." He watched for the older man's reaction. Malone didn't even blink.

He tried again.

"I did as you suggested and went to the courthouse and checked the records." Jake took a deep breath and braced himself. "Monty Summers is my son, isn't he, even though Dale is listed as the father?"

The old man nodded. "Yes."

"How did you know?"

Malone sighed.

"I've carried that secret around with me all these years. I never told anyone, not even my wife." He frowned. "The last time I saw you and Marilyn, you were sitting in a booth in my drive-in, listening to the jukebox." The old man smiled, his eyes lighting at the memory. "The two of you reminded me of myself and my sweet Bertha when we were courting."

Jake shifted in his chair, anxious to hear the details.

"Anyway," Malone continued, "you two sat in that booth, playing the same song over and over." Malone scratched his head. "It was 'Only You,' by The Platters, if I remember right."

Jake shook his head. "You remember that after all these years?"

Malone grinned. "You two played it so much that night I almost memorized the words. The next day, I heard some of the other kids say you'd left to follow the harvest. I remember thinking you were awful brave to leave that little girl.

"About a month later, I'd stepped out for a breath of fresh air before I cleaned and locked up for the night. Dale Summers pulled in and parked close to the back door where I was standing, in that shiny new car his folks had bought him for graduation. He had a girl with him, but I couldn't see her face."

The old man crossed his bony legs. "The car windows were down, and I could hear him talking to her. Summers kept saying everything would be okay, but this girl kept crying and saying her daddy wanted her to get rid of the baby."

Jake recoiled as though he had been struck. Old man Baker had always been harsh and strait-laced, but killing an unborn baby? He walked to the fireplace, his back to Malone. He couldn't bear to look him in the face while the old man finished his story.

"Right in the middle of her crying, Dale told her they would get married."

Jake flinched. Struggling for control, he gripped the mantle.

"Are you okay?"

Jake swallowed the bitter taste in his mouth and nodded. "I'm fine. Keep talking."

"As I said, Dale said they would get married. He said he'd claim the baby was his, but the girl objected. She said she loved you, and I realized your Marilyn was in the car. At that point, I forgot all about not eavesdropping and started listening closer. Dale said, 'When Jake comes home, we'll get the marriage annulled. It's the only way we can save the baby's life.'"

An involuntary moan escaped Jake's lips. It came from a place deep inside him, where it had hidden since the day he'd received Kay's note about the marriage. Malone stopped talking. Jake closed his eyes and tried to breathe normally. "Go on."

"It was all over town that Marilyn had eloped with Summers. Her folks disowned her. Local gossips said you'd run out on her, but I didn't believe it. I knew how much you loved that little girl. Something had to have happened to keep you away. I prayed you'd come back, but as the years passed, I lost hope. When you showed up in town a few weeks ago, I decided that somehow you had to know you had a son before you left again. I wanted you to find out for yourself. It wasn't my place to tell you."

Jake stumbled back to his chair and sat down. He buried his face in his hands, tears streaming down his cheeks. He'd put Marilyn through so much needless pain. They hadn't betrayed him at all. They'd done the only thing they knew to do to protect the baby. *His son.*

A gentle hand touched his shoulder.

"I'm sorry, son. I know it's painful for you, but you had the right to know. I couldn't imagine how all this changed your life, but I could see the pain in your eyes every time we talked. That's why I kept coming back, encouraging you to go see Summers. The Good Book says 'Ye shall know the truth and the truth shall make you free.' Let God free you from the pain of the past."

Jake didn't know how long he sat in that chair. Time seemed to stand still as he let go of the bitterness and anger he'd mistakenly held for so long. In his emotional agony, his lips couldn't form the words for prayer. His heart did the praying for him, asking for grace and forgiveness.

When at last he raised his head, he felt drained, but somehow lighter. A weight had lifted, but a new pain had taken its place. He hadn't been betrayed by Dale and Marilyn—he'd left them in a situation with no way out. They had done the best they could under the circumstances.

Only one question remained:

Could he make things right, or was it too late?

CHAPTER 22

MONDAY, JUNE 21ST, 6:00 P.M.

Jake's first thought after talking with Carl Malone was to find Marilyn. Now that he knew the truth, he longed to be with her again, but feared she might feel nothing for him. She would be at the hospital with her son—no, *their* son. He couldn't just walk into the hospital and announce he was ready to become the father of a twenty-four-year-old. For one thing, Monty believed Dale was his father. And Dale had raised a son he loved like his own.

What he could do was visit Dale. He pulled the truck into the hospital parking lot and climbed the steps to the front door. The same gray-haired woman sat behind the lobby desk, and she smiled as he approached.

"Mr. Reynolds, it's good to see you again. What can I do for you today?"

An idea flickered through Jake's mind. "Can Monty Summers have visitors yet?"

The receptionist checked her patient roster and shook her head.

"I'm sorry, only family is allowed in. I'd think *you'd* be able to visit him, since you donated the blood he needed, but ..." She gave him an apologetic smile.

Jake nodded. "I understand." He wondered what she'd think if she knew he was family. "What about the other Mr. Summers?"

"Oh, yes, there you're in luck. Room 110. Follow this hall all the way to the end and take a left."

A few seconds later, Jake stood before the door to Dale's room. He took a deep breath, and before he had a chance to change his mind, he knocked.

"Come in."

Jake pushed open the door.

Dale let his magazine drop. Recognition started in his eyes and turned into a slow smile.

"Jake?"

Jake nodded. He couldn't seem to get his voice to work. All the things he'd planned to say, the questions he'd carried, all of it escaped him. Images flashed in his mind—the two of them fishing and skinny dipping in Miller's Creek. Riding in Dale's '57 Chevy. Double dating with Marilyn and Kay. How had so many years gone by?

Dale stood.

"Been a long time. I'm glad you decided to come."

Jake closed the door, but didn't come any farther. "I heard you're doing better."

Dale shrugged. "Doc Ashworth thinks I'm gonna make it."

"That's good."

Silence filled the room.

Dale took a sip of water from a glass on the table.

"You're living in Atlanta?"

"Yes."

Silence again. Jake wondered if he had made a mistake by coming, but he had too many questions that needed answers to leave now.

"I got your note," he finally said. Dale indicated the chair in the corner.

"Have a seat."

Jake moved the chair closer and sat down, while Dale eased himself down into the recliner beside the bed. He blew his breath out in a long, ragged sigh as though he might be nervous.

"There's so much I want to say, but I don't know where to begin." He rubbed his hand across his face, blew his breath out again, and finally looked up. "Why did you wait so long to come back? You were only going to be away for the summer."

The question sounded like an accusation. Anger briefly threatened below the surface of Jake's feelings, but he pushed it away. Dale studied him for a moment, and then spoke again.

"Sorry. I guess that question is irrelevant now. I'm sure you had your reasons." He ran his hand through his hair. "Kay tells me your aunt Nora's house burned night before last. I'm sorry to hear that. You came back at a bad time."

"You got that right. But I didn't have a lot of choice in the matter."

"James Sheridan isn't one for giving people a choice."

Jake wondered how much Dale knew about recent events. "Have you heard about the shooting?"

Dale nodded.

"Attempted murder is a terrible thing, but maybe it was the only way to stop him. He's tearing this town apart."

Silence invaded the room again. Jake glanced over at Dale, who squirmed in his chair as though trying to find a comfortable position. *Come on, man, let's get this over with.*

Dale cleared his throat and coughed.

"Kay told me you would be here for only a short time. I wanted to see you before you left." He coughed again and cleared his throat. "I thought I was going to die when I had the heart attack. I was afraid of what lay beyond death. I thought about my life, and about all the things I've left undone over the years."

He fidgeted with the belt on his robe. "The thing I regretted most was the loss of our friendship, and not being able to see you again, to tell you what happened that summer."

Jake laced his fingers together and tried to relax. It was what he had come to hear, but his chest still felt heavy, as though something weighed it down.

Dale looked him in the eye. "I'm sure you've believed all these years that Marilyn and I double-crossed you, but we had a good reason for what we did." He closed his eyes but continued speaking. "I made you a promise the night before you left. I told you I would take care of Marilyn." Dale opened his eyes and shook his head. "You have no idea how those words have haunted me."

Jake knew he could save Dale the stress of explaining the details, but he also knew Dale needed to say what was on his mind as much as he needed to hear it. His insides were a pulsating bundle of nerves.

"After you left town, I didn't know what to do with myself. You were the brother I never had, and I missed the heck out of you.

"I was so lonesome that summer. I spent a lot of time going to all our old haunts, but it wasn't the same." He stopped for a moment and looked at Jake. "One night I was driving around town, killing time. I saw Marilyn walking down Sycamore Street. It was getting late, so I stopped and asked if she wanted a ride home."

Dale exhaled a deep breath and shook his head. "When she got in the car, I couldn't believe my eyes. She was crying, all beat up, blood on her clothes. Scared me out of my wits. I thought somebody'd attacked her."

Jake concentrated on breathing slowly to control his nausea at Dale's words. He studied the other man's face, and saw pain and weary anguish.

"If you're tired," Jake said, "I can come back another time."

Dale opened his eyes.

"No. I've waited a long time to tell you these things. You need to hear this, in case something should happen to me." He gripped the arms of the chair with white-knuckled hands. "When I asked Marilyn what happened, she blurted it all out. Her old man hit her after he found out she was pregnant."

Jake cringed, closing his eyes against the image of Marilyn's father punishing her for his mistake. Because of him, she'd suffered.

If only I had resisted and not given in to my passion that night. If only I hadn't left her here alone. If only ...

They were both quiet for a moment.

Dale sighed. "I know how much you two loved each other. What you did is your business, but the consequences cost all of us."

Jake squirmed in his chair. It was one thing to know he'd done something wrong. To have others suffer because of his actions and then confront him with it was beyond humiliating.

Dale stared at Jake for several moments, but his eyes held no resentment or accusation.

"Monty is your son, Jake."

Jake swallowed the lump building in his throat and said, "Why didn't you let me know?"

Dale threw up his hands as if in surrender. "We didn't know where you were, and we didn't have time to hunt you down. Her old man had arranged for an abortion because he was worried about his image, his good name. Didn't care that it was illegal. I absolutely could not let that happen to my best friend's girl or his baby, and marriage seemed to be our only way out." He heaved a weary-sounding sigh. "I wasn't in love with Marilyn. Don't get me wrong, I was fond of her, but it was never even close to what the two of you had."

Jake gave him the briefest of nods to indicate he understood, and Dale continued.

"Looking back on it now, it's hard to believe that we did what we did. The next day, we drove to Austin, checked into a motel room, did the blood test and the three-day wait. Then we found a JP, who agreed to marry us after I slipped him some extra money. So during the time Marilyn was supposed to be getting an abortion, we were getting married. Afterward, I called my dad and asked him to let her folks know. When things cooled down, we came back to town and moved in with my parents."

He looked up at Jake. "Marilyn's old man was *so* mad. He showed up at the house, and my dad had to call the sheriff to get rid of him. Marilyn never did give in to him. She stood her ground. Her mom and dad moved away not long after that, so they never saw their grandchild."

Jake took a minute to digest the information. He walked to the window and looked at the hospital parking lot simmering under the Texas sun before turning back to Dale.

"Why didn't you get hold of me when things cooled down?"

"We tried. I went to your house, but your dad threw me out. Called me a traitor and a few other choice names. Threatened to call the law if I didn't leave."

"When did this happen?"

"A month or so after we married. Your dad shoved that old shotgun of his in my face. Your mother was crying and taking on like somebody died. Said she didn't want her son involved in any scandal.

"When they wouldn't help us, we went to see your aunt Nora. She said we'd done enough damage already, and we should leave you alone. Marilyn started crying and told her about the baby, and swore her to secrecy. She eventually gave us the last address she had for you. Marilyn wrote to you that night, to let you know why we got married."

Jake's stomach churned at the memory of burning the letter. If he'd had nerve enough to read it, they could all have been spared a lot of hurt.

Dale massaged his temples with his fingertips. "I kept looking for you to come home that first year." He looked up, his eyes glassy with weariness. "Why didn't you come back?"

"Kay wrote me that the two of you had gotten married. I didn't know anything about the pregnancy. I was so angry, I never bothered to read the letter from Marilyn. I burned it."

Dale reached for the glass again and sipped some water.

"Our original plan was to get an annulment, so the two of you could marry when you came home. It wasn't the best plan in the world, but what else could we do? We were two scared kids trying to fix a problem."

He gave Jake a long look. "I was mad at you for a long time. I thought you'd run out on her, and on me too for that matter. I never figured you for that kind of guy."

"But you stayed married."

"Out of necessity. I didn't even kiss her when we got married." Dale smiled. "You should have seen the look on that JP's face when I refused to kiss the bride." He grew somber again. "As far as I was concerned, Marilyn belonged to you. We even slept in separate rooms." He looked down for a moment, then shook his head. "I had a hard time explaining that one to my folks. But when they found out she was pregnant, they didn't ask any more questions."

Jake's face grew warm at the realization of what these two people had endured because of him. Marilyn had been forced into a relationship with another man, and Dale had given up his own future to protect her and the baby.

Dale looked out the window and his eyes had a faraway look as if he were somewhere else.

"When Monty turned two years old, I gave up on you and moved into her room. Without an invitation, I might add. I tried to tell myself she was my wife, but I could never shake the guilt I felt."

He sighed. "She wasn't in love with me, Jake. She never has been, but she was a good wife and mother. We loved each other as family, but we weren't in love. She stayed until Monty graduated from high school. Then she moved out."

Jake frowned. "It never occurred to you that I'd found out about the marriage, and that's why I didn't come back?"

"Never crossed my mind. We didn't know Kay had been in touch with you. After Monty was born, we concentrated on raising him." Dale ran his hand across his face, resignation evident in his eyes. "I love that boy as if he were my own. All the same, he's your boy, Jake."

An incredible feeling crept over Jake. It had taken a lot for Dale to admit Monty wasn't his. But if not for this man, his son wouldn't be alive.

"Jake, I hope you can forgive me for everything that's happened."

Jake heard the tremor in Dale's voice, and then heard Carl Malone's words.

Peace only comes to them that make peace.

"No. I'm the one who should be apologizing to you." A lump formed in Jake's throat, but he forced himself to finish. "I guess we all had our reasons for what we did. I know I did, and you and Marilyn suffered for it. I'm sorry for that."

He stood and held out his hand to his childhood friend. "Thank you for saving my son's life." He tried to blink back the hot tears that stung his eyes.

Dale grasped Jake's hand and pulled him into a hug. The two men clung to each other, tears streaming down their cheeks.

"Welcome home, Jake."

Peace enveloped Jake, even as he wondered if Marilyn would feel the same way.

CHAPTER 23

Morning sunlight streamed through the window and danced on Monty's pale face. Marilyn leaned over and kissed his forehead.

"Good morning, Monty. Did you sleep well?" She wasn't sure he could hear her, but Dr. Ashworth had encouraged her to talk to him.

"Your dad is so much better. He's been moved from ICU and may go home soon. Isn't that good news?" Marilyn patted Monty's arm, then walked to the window to gaze out into the sun-drenched morning.

"Mom?"

The voice was so soft, Marilyn thought she was hearing things. She turned to see Monty's eyelids flutter open. She hurried to his side.

"Monty!" She squeezed his hand and reached for the buzzer to alert the nurse. "It's so good to see you open your eyes."

A nurse hurried in with Dr. Ashworth close behind. He took one look at his patient and began checking vital signs. After a few moments, he straightened, a smile on his face. "How are you feeling, young man?"

Monty looked around the room, a puzzled expression on his face.

"What is it, Monty?" Dr. Ashworth asked.

"Why am I here?"

The doctor looked puzzled. "Don't you remember?"

"No."

Dr. Ashworth glanced at Marilyn. Her heart sank. Had Monty lost his memory? No of course not. He knew her.

The doctor laid his hand on the young man's shoulder. "You were brought in with a gunshot wound. Can you remember anything about being shot?"

Monty surveyed the room as if seeking his memory. Marilyn watched understanding dawn on his face.

He nodded. "Sheridan. He shot me." He frowned. "Did they catch him?"

Dr. Ashworth patted his shoulder. "Don't worry about Mr. Sheridan right now. We'll talk more later." He motioned for Marilyn to follow him.

"I'd like to stay with my son."

Dr. Ashworth nodded. "I understand. This won't take but a minute."

"But ..."

He moved toward the door. Marilyn sighed, then gave Monty a quick kiss before following the doctor into the hall.

Dr. Ashworth smiled. "Looks like we have our boy back." He shook his head. "I've heard of this happening with comatose patients. They sometimes awaken as if they've been taking a nap. But I've never experienced it in my practice before."

"Is he going to be okay?"

"I believe so. His vitals are good, and he remembered the shooting incident. But we need to avoid too much excitement. Don't let him overdo the talking. He still needs plenty of rest to make a complete recovery."

Marilyn hugged the doctor. "Thank you," she said. "I can't tell you how grateful I am to have my son back."

"It wasn't my doing," the doctor said, and gave her a huge smile. "As far as I'm concerned, we've got us a bona fide miracle in that bed."

Jake awoke for the first time in twenty-five years feeling good about life. No more bitterness. He felt clean, somehow. Somewhere, sometime in between his visit to Carl Malone and then to Dale, the burden of hard feelings had all seeped away. He bathed, shaved, and dressed, whistling to himself the whole time.

He walked down the hall and tapped on Mr. Woods's door, still whistling.

"Morning, Mr. Woods."

"My, you're chipper this morning. What kind of tonic are you taking?"

He patted the older man on the back and smiled. "It's called peace of mind."

Mr. Woods nodded and smiled. "Sit down and tell me about it. The biscuits and coffee are almost ready."

Tuesday, June 22nd, 10:00 a.m.

The door to Dale's room stood open, but Kay knocked anyway before she entered. She wanted to say hello before she went to work.

Dale, in street clothes, looked up from his half-full suitcase and smiled. "Good morning."

His smile still sent shivers up her spine after all these years. The scent of his aftershave floated across the room to greet her.

She dropped her purse into a nearby chair. "You're looking fit."

His smile grew wider. "I have good reason."

"Let me guess. You're going home."

"Yes, Doc came by earlier and said I could leave if I took it easy." He placed a pair of pajamas in the suitcase, the smile still playing around his lips. "The real reason I feel so good is because Jake came to see me."

Kay squealed and threw her arms around his neck, hugging him. "That's the best news I've heard in weeks."

Dale's arms slid around her, returning her hug. For a moment, Kay held her breath. She let her arms fall from his neck and tried to step back, but Dale pulled her close.

He laughed. "You don't think you're going to get away that easily, do you?" He raised her chin until their eyes met, and then he leaned closer and brushed a kiss across her lips. "That's for taking such good care of me for the past few days."

As he went back to his packing, Kay clasped her hands together to keep them from trembling. *Lord, help me here. I don't know what to say.*

Dale dropped his robe into the suitcase. When he glanced up and saw how pale and uncertain her face had become, he stopped packing.

"Was I out of line? We've known each other a long time. I just wanted to show you my appreciation for all you've done."

"No." She fidgeted with the bracelets on her arm. "Actually, I rather enjoyed it."

Dale looked surprised, then pleased. "To be truthful, I did too." He looked puzzled. "Why haven't we spent any time together since ... you know?"

She hesitated, wondering how much she should reveal.

"Do you remember the fight Marilyn and I had, after you and she got married?" She waved a hand in a dismissive gesture. "I know it's been a long time ago. You might not recall it."

Dale nodded. "Yes, I do. You two didn't speak for years after that." He frowned. "I never could get Marilyn to tell me what happened."

"That's because the fight was about you."

"You're kidding!"

Kay saw the shock spread across his face. "It's true."

"You mean it was my fault the two of you ...?" He paused, realization dawning in his eyes. "You were *jealous*?"

Kay nodded. "It was more than jealousy. Marilyn knew my true feelings way before the two of you had to get married."

"Whoa. Wait a minute." Dale held up a hand. "What do you mean, 'had to get married'?" When she was silent, he sighed, and the hand dropped.

"Of course that's what you thought. That's what everyone in town thought." He sat down on the side of the bed and patted the spot next to him. She eased down onto the bed, glad to get off her shaking legs.

Dale squeezed her hand. "I'm going to share a secret with you, but you have to keep it to yourself. Agreed?"

She nodded. "Agreed."

Dale inhaled and then let out his breath. He hesitated a moment before speaking. "Monty's not my son. I married Marilyn to protect her and the child she was carrying."

Shock coursed through Kay. "Then whose—" She stopped as the puzzle pieces fell together in her mind. *Of course.* "Jake?"

Dale nodded. "He's Monty's biological father."

"And Jake knows?"

He nodded again. "I told him last night."

"How'd he take it?"

Dale shrugged. "Last night, at least, he seemed okay with the idea. He didn't say too much. That's a big thing to take in all at once."

He squeezed her hand again. "Hey, enough about Jake and Marilyn. Let's go back to talking about us." He caressed the back of her hand, rubbing his thumb across it. "What about those feelings you were talking about?"

Kay looked down at their intertwined hands. "Marilyn knew I was interested in you—more than interested."

"How come you never let on? The four of us double-dated all through high school."

She gave him a weak smile. "We were all best friends, and we were always together. It was never just you and me. You never gave any indication you were interested in anything more. Then Jake left, and a few weeks later, all of a sudden you and Marilyn eloped. I knew there would never be a chance for us."

"But she and I have been divorced five years now." He grinned. "You could have let me know something before then."

"Too much time had passed."

"Don't think I didn't like you back then. My reason for not getting more involved was because my dad told me if I didn't go to college he would disinherit me." Dale laughed. "He sure made a believer out of me.

"I knew marriage was out of the question until I got my degree, so I never said anything. I thought we had all kinds of time. Little did I know that Jake and Marilyn were going to change all of our lives. When my dad found out she and I were married, he almost had a stroke, until I told him Marilyn was pregnant."

"But you could have told me ..."

Dale placed his finger against her lips. "Shhh. When I married Marilyn, we agreed it would be a temporary thing. I had no idea then that Jake wouldn't come home. And afterward, so much time passed I couldn't make up my mind to pursue a relationship again."

Kay sighed. "I understand."

"But now," he said, and slipped his arm around her to pull her closer, "it looks like we have a lot of lost time to make up for."

She opened her mouth to answer him, but his kiss muffled her words.

Marilyn stopped short at the sight of the two people in Dale's hospital room sharing an embrace. She moved to back out of the room and promptly bumped her elbow hard on the door jamb.

"Ouch!"

Dale and Kay jerked apart and turned toward her.

"Pardon the interruption." Marilyn rubbed her elbow and gave the couple a good-humored snippy look. "*Well.* It certainly took you two long enough."

Dale smiled. "Next time, knock."

"Anyway, I'm happy for you." Marilyn looked from one to the other. Kay blushed and glanced away, and Dale shrugged.

"We forgive you. Come on in."

Marilyn closed the door. "If I didn't have such good news, I wouldn't stay, but the reason I'm here is because of Monty."

"Yeah, what about Monty?" Dale frowned. "Where is that boy anyway? I haven't seen him in days. I tried calling the house several times, but he's never home."

Marilyn nodded. "It's a long story, but you've been too ill for me to let you know." And for the next twenty minutes, she filled Dale in on the details of Monty's gunshot and subsequent coma.

"I knew there'd been a shooting," Dale said. "I overheard two of the nurses talking about it. I had no idea it was Monty."

"It was pretty touch-and-go for a while," Marilyn said. "He needed a transfusion, and the hospital had fits with his blood type. They gave him what they had, but then they couldn't get hold of any more. Then a donor showed up."

Dale looked puzzled, then nodded. "You know who that donor had to be."

"The doctor said the donor preferred to remain anonymous. I'm just thankful someone cared enough to do that for Monty."

Dale smiled. "You *know* it had to be Jake."

Marilyn kept talking to cover her emotions. "Well, whoever it was, Monty's awake now, and you're stronger, so I thought it was time you heard. Dr. Ashworth told me he's releasing you today, and I didn't want you to hear it on the street."

Dale stood and hugged her. "I'm glad our boy is going to be okay."

Kay nodded. "Yes, we're both glad to hear that Monty's better. And Dale has some good news of his own."

Now it was Marilyn's turn to look puzzled. "You do?"

Dale nodded. "Jake came to see me."

Marilyn's smile faded and her heart pounded. "I thought Jake didn't want anything to do with either one of us."

Dale shrugged. "I don't know what changed his mind, but he showed up yesterday." He patted her arm. "It's okay. I explained everything to him and he's all right with it. The past is finally behind us."

Marilyn's chest felt as though it were caught in a vise. She struggled to breathe and felt as though she might faint. Before they could say anything else, she turned and hurried from the room.

Marilyn rushed to her car, her breath coming in short gasps. She sank onto the car seat and laid her head against the headrest.

She needed a place to be alone and think. She started the engine and headed east out of town. A few moments later, she pulled into Pearce's Lookout and parked, and then walked to the edge of the rise overlooking Archer Springs.

The familiar memory came rushing toward her like a springtime thunderstorm, catching her up in its fury before she could hide from it. Marilyn closed her eyes and let the memory storm carry her into its center.

She had trusted Jake not to hurt her. As they sat in the car and talked, she couldn't stop her tears. The tenderness of his touch made the tears worse. Then she felt his lips on hers, and she'd allowed herself to become immersed in his love.

The next day, shame and guilt enveloped her. When she finally realized she was pregnant, she went to church with her mother and begged God not to let it be so. The minister's sermon terrified her. He read a verse from the Bible that said her sin would find her out. She was convinced it already had.

Marilyn took a deep breath, pushed the memory away, and tried to calm her frazzled nerves. This wasn't all her doing. She wouldn't be here on this hillside, full of humiliation and pain, if Jake had come home as he'd promised.

Who do you think you are, Jake, coming back after all this time? I needed you then. I trusted you then, but you broke your promise.

The intense mid-afternoon heat brought her back to reality as sweat drizzled down her neck. Marilyn trudged to the car, climbed in, and heaved a long sigh. She couldn't blame Dale for talking to Jake, wanting to be free of the self-imposed secrecy and guilt he'd carried through the years. He felt he'd betrayed his best friend. In reality, Jake had betrayed them by disappearing from their lives and leaving them to deal with the aftermath of their mistake. He'd forced her and Dale into a relationship that neither wanted.

Marilyn drove back toward Archer Springs, her heart heavy. There was only one solution to this chaos. Only one way to protect Monty, to keep Jake from walking out on Monty like he had her.

She would have to avoid Jake at all costs.

CHAPTER 24

Jake shoveled another load of the burned remains of Aunt Nora's house onto the borrowed trailer, then wiped his forehead with the back of his hand. The sweltering heat added to his physical discomfort, but nothing could dampen his excitement at knowing he had a son.

As he threw another shovelful onto the trailer bed, he heard a car horn. Kay climbed out of her car, smiling and waving like her old self. She'd been despondent while Dale and Monty had been in the hospital. It was good to see her happy again.

She rushed to him and, before he could stop her, threw her arms around his waist and hugged him.

He laughed. "Now what would make a pretty woman like you hug a dirty sweaty man like me?"

"Dale told me the two of you worked things out yesterday. You don't know how happy that makes me."

Jake grinned. "I'm pretty happy about it myself. I feel like I've been given a second chance at life."

Kay grew serious. "Are you going to tell Monty you're his father?"

Jake leaned on his shovel. "As much as I'd like to get to know him, I'm afraid it's something that will have to wait. He believes Dale is his father. I don't want to spoil that."

He shook his head. "Believe me, since yesterday I've gone over every possibility, and I haven't yet come up with a solution."

"I'd say it wouldn't be spoiling anything." Kay smiled at Jake. "The guy has two great fathers."

He scooped another shovelful of rubble onto the trailer. "There are others to consider besides myself. Monty's been through a traumatic time with the shooting. There's also Marilyn to consider. I don't know how she feels."

Kay dabbed at her damp forehead with a tissue. "Dale told her yesterday that you and he had talked."

"And?"

"She just looked like she'd seen a ghost and ran out of the room."

Jake sighed. "I was afraid of that. Can't much blame her." He pushed some charred lumber into a pile. "I may have to be content with knowing Monty through Dale. I think for now we should leave things as they are."

"Is that what you want?"

Jake shrugged. "Do I have a choice?"

Later, as he watched her drive away, one thought was uppermost in his mind:

What I want is to have my family together.

Dale Summers pushed open the door to his son's hospital room. Monty appeared to be asleep, but he opened his eyes and smiled when Dale touched his shoulder.

"Hi, Dad. You okay?"

Dale nodded. "Doc released me this morning. I'm on my way home." He walked to the foot of the bed and surveyed the bandages covering Monty's chest. "From what I understand, you had a close call."

Monty nodded. "You know what happened?"

"Only that Sheridan shot you, but I don't know why. Feel like talking about it?"

Monty took a deep breath.

"I thought Sheridan was a good person. You and the other men on the city council seemed to like him. He wanted what was best for Archer Springs, or at least I thought he did. He offered me a lot of money to work for him. I thought it was my chance to get out on my own, buy my own place."

Dale remained at the foot of the bed without speaking.

"He started out asking me to do little jobs for him."

Dale gripped the bed rail. "What kind of jobs?"

"Phone calls to threaten people into selling their property to him. He didn't want anyone to recognize his voice. One time, he asked me to vandalize an old house on Orchard Street. Some guy had come to town and started remodeling the house. Sheridan was hotter than blue blazes about it. So I went over there and sprayed red paint on the walls. It didn't stop the guy, though. He repainted and moved in."

Dale cringed at the address. It had to be Jake's house.

"The clincher came when he asked me to burn that same house. I couldn't do it, Dad. I couldn't. When I was a kid, I used to go to that old house when I wanted to be alone. It was deserted, but for some reason, I always felt safe there." He looked away from Dale for a moment. "I never told you or Mom that I went there.""

Dale flinched again. Monty couldn't know the house belonged to Jake, and yet he'd taken refuge there. He seemed to be discovering a lot of new things about the boy he'd raised. Maybe he hadn't been as good a father as he'd thought.

Monty continued. "One day, I drove by with a Molotov cocktail ..." He paused, shame coloring his face again. "I'm sorry, Dad. I have to get this out of my system."

Dale walked to the side of the bed and laid his hand on Monty's shoulder.

"No one understands any better than I do about getting something out of your system. It hurts me to know you were mixed up with somebody like Sheridan, but I'm glad you can tell me about it. Keep going."

"Sheridan wanted me to set the house on fire."

Dale's heart lurched.

"Monty, were you responsible for any of those other house fires?"

"No, that wasn't me. I don't know who did the actual burning of those houses, but it wasn't me. I did drive by the house on Orchard with a Molotov to throw, but when I got even with the house, someone was on the front porch. When I saw him, I couldn't do it."

"Thank God you didn't, Son."

"I've never been so scared in all my life. I went to Sheridan and told him I wanted out. He pulled a gun on me. I took off running, and he shot me, and that's the last thing I remember until I woke up here."

Dale shoved his hands in his pockets and pretended to gaze out the window, wondering how much he should tell Monty.

"What about Sheridan?" Monty said. "Did they lock him up?"

Dale turned back to the bed. "No, Son, he's here in the hospital under guard. Someone shot him."

"For real?"

Dale nodded. "They don't know who did it yet, but they know it was a woman. A witness overheard them arguing, and saw her come running out of the office with a gun. In the dark, the only thing he noticed was her ponytail. Apparently Sheridan and this woman were having an affair, and he dumped her."

The color drained from Monty's face. Dale frowned.

"Do you feel okay? You need the nurse?"

Monty shook his head. "No, no. I'm all right."

"Then what is it? Have I talked too much? I should go and let you rest." Dale started for the door, but Monty's words stopped him cold.

"It's Clara Mae, Dad."

Dale turned and looked at Monty.

"What did you say?"

Monty took a deep breath.

"Clara Mae and Sheridan were having an affair. They'd sneak off to those sleazy old motel rooms in Woodson. She wears her hair in a ponytail sometimes. Clara Mae had to have been who shot Sheridan."

Dale hung up the phone and leaned back in the leather recliner. The sheriff had explained everything. He still found it hard to believe his own cousin had shot Sheridan, but when the sheriff searched her apartment he found the gun hidden in a drawer full of lingerie, along with pictures of her and Sheridan. She not only confessed to the shooting, but also to starting several fires, including the one that torched Jake's house. And she admitted borrowing Monty's Volkswagen every time she went out to set a fire. Sheridan had convinced her to do it all by promising her a future.

She was in jail. Dale sighed. Poor Clara Mae. She never seemed to learn from her mistakes.

CHAPTER 25

Jake took a long swig from a thermos of ice water. Only a few more shovels full, and he would be finished. He reached down and picked up a wooden slat, the only remnant of the porch swing, and something flashed in the bright sunlight. He knelt and picked it up. His heart leapt into his throat as he gazed at a long-lost promise. Half a golden heart on a slender gold chain.

Jake rubbed the burn smut off the heart pendant with his thumb. It shone as brightly as it did on the night he'd placed it around Marilyn's neck. He guessed the slat from the swing must have kept it from being damaged, but how on earth did it get here? The last time he'd seen it, it was in the treasure chest. Jake's mind flashed back to the night of the fire. He had stumbled over the chest going out the front door. The chain must have fallen out when he picked up the chest.

He slipped the chain in his jeans pocket but couldn't stop thinking about it. The pendant had survived for twenty-five years in an attic, and then managed to come through a fire without being tarnished.

That's how love should be, shouldn't it? Untarnished by whatever fire you put it through.

He finished shoveling and gazed at the empty lot. A part of his childhood, his legacy, was gone. What now? Did he stay in Archer Springs, since his son was here, or did he go back to Atlanta? He had no job there, no significant other, only an empty apartment. Thinking about it depressed him. Maybe it was time to make a fresh start. Maybe he could make that happen here in Archer Springs.

Later that evening, when Jake arrived at the motel, Mr. Woods greeted him.

"Hey there, Jake. How's the clean-up going?"

"It's finished." Jake stretched his tired muscles.

The old man squinted at Jake and cocked his head to one side.

"Have you got a minute? I know you're tired, but I got something to talk to you about."

"Sure." Jake leaned against the doorframe leading to the hallway, every muscle and joint aching for relief. He couldn't wait to soak in a hot bath.

"Jake, it doesn't take a smart person to know I'm not going to be around much longer. I've lived a good long life, and I don't have regrets, but I've been thinking about something the past few days." The old man scratched his head as if deciding what to say next. "Since you don't have a job to go back to, why don't you stay here and run this motel?"

Jake looked at the older man in surprise.

"Now, I don't want to put any pressure on you," Mr. Woods said, "but I'm offering to sell you this business. You won't get rich, but you'll have a place to live, and during the summer months you'll make enough profit to carry you the rest of the year." The old man paused and chewed on his lip for a moment. "I only have one stipulation. I don't have any family to stay with, so I'd like to live here until I pass on."

Jake frowned. "Are you sure about this? This place has been your whole life."

"I'm sure. I been thinking about it a lot, and I don't want to sell to just any rustler that walks through the door." He smiled a hopeful, elfin smile. "But I'd be mighty pleased to sell it to you."

Jake closed his eyes. He needed time to mull it over.

"This is kind of sudden. Could I have a day or two to think it through?"

"Of course. Take all the time you like. I'm not offering it to anyone else right now."

That evening, soaking in a steaming tub, Jake let his mind dwell on the possibilities of life in Archer Springs. There was his friendship with Dale, living and growing anew. There was his newfound son, an idea that appealed to him. And there was the small-town slower pace. Aside from houses burning down and people getting shot, it had started to feel like home. And Archer Springs would be even quieter now that Sheridan and Clara Mae had been stopped.

He did have one reservation. He didn't know how Marilyn would feel about him staying here, and getting acquainted with Monty.

Jake slid farther down into the steaming water.

The only way to find out is try and see.

FRIDAY, JUNE 25TH, 9:00 A.M.

The next morning, Jake knocked on Jonathan Woods's door.

"How soon do you want me to take over?"

The old man grinned. "How about right now?"

Jake filled their coffee cups and joined him at the table. "You *are* in a hurry, aren't you?"

Mr. Woods chuckled.

"I'm not getting any younger, Jake, and the fish are calling me."

Jake laughed along with the old man.

"Okay, you've got yourself a deal. We can get the paperwork started today if you want. I just hope I can do as good a job as you've done all these years."

"You'll do fine, my boy. I'll be right here to show you the ropes and help you get started."

After their talk, Jake walked out on the porch of the motel with his third cup of coffee. Clouds obscured the sun, and for a change, a breeze ruffled his hair and teased the leaves on the lone tree standing beside the building.

A late model silver Ford pickup stopped in front of the motel, and Dale climbed out. He waved in Jake's direction. At five feet, six inches, Dale wasn't a tall man, but the old Summers swagger was still evident in his walk as he strode for the porch. Clad in boots, jeans, and a Stetson, an air of confidence swirled around him. Jake smiled. It was the Dale he remembered.

Dale stepped onto the porch. "Good morning." He stood there looking at Jake for a moment.

A feeling of uneasiness crept over Jake. "Something wrong?"

Dale shook his head. "I can't get over the fact you're here after all these years. Have I told you how good it is to have you back?"

Jake nodded. "It feels pretty good to me too." He took a sip of coffee and studied the man in front of him. "I didn't plan on things turning out this way."

Dale kicked at a loose board on the porch. "Can I ask you something?"

"What's on your mind?"

"Got a proposition for you."

Jake laughed. "Do I have a sign on my back asking for propositions?"

Dale grinned and pretended to look at Jake's back. He shook his head. "I don't see one. Are you getting a lot of offers these days?"

"It does look like I'll be staying in Archer Springs."

"That's great." Dale slapped Jake on the shoulder. "It'll be like old times having you around. What made you decide to stay?"

"I'm buying the motel. Mr. Woods wants to spend the rest of his days on the creek bank, and I'm ready to give up big city life."

"Well, shucks. I was going to ask you about working with me in my real estate business." Dale patted his chest. "Doc says I have to slow down, take it easy for a while."

"Me?" Jake shook his head. "I don't know anything about real estate."

"You don't have to. I'll take care of all the legal work and the actual selling. I need someone to assist me with farm listings and acreage, not anything that requires a license. How about it?" He grinned. "Monty's decided to get his license, so we'd all be working together."

Jake shook his head. "I'm going to have my hands full learning the ropes of motel operation. I don't know about handling two new jobs. What about Kay? Maybe she can help you. I won't need her as much as Mr. Woods did."

Dale snapped his fingers. "Good thinking. I could use her in the office." He grinned. "She might be too much of a distraction, but I could still use you." He pushed his Stetson farther back on his head. "Tell you what. You get started in the motel business, and once you've got the hang of it, then you can come in with me. How does that sound?"

Jake laughed. "Yesterday I didn't even have a job. Today I have two."

CHAPTER 26

FRIDAY, JUNE 25TH, 5:00 P.M.

Jake needed to go back to Atlanta for his furniture and personal possessions, but he hated to go alone now he'd made the decision to stay in Archer Springs. Atlanta seemed like another time and place, and he wanted to get on with his life here. When Dale came back later with burgers for lunch, Jake told him about his plans.

"I'm trying to decide when to go to Atlanta to move my belongings here, but I'm dreading the trip."

"Well, why don't I go with you? It would give us a chance to catch up on what we've been doing with our lives since ..." He didn't finish the sentence, but he didn't have to. Not with Jake.

"I don't know, Dale. You're recovering from a heart attack. Are you sure you're up to riding that far?" Jake raised an eyebrow. "I don't want to have to give you CPR. What's the doctor going to say about you going with me?"

Dale shoved his hands into his jeans. "Do we have to tell him?"

"I think it would be a good idea to get his opinion."

Dale laughed.

"Okay, I'll call him this afternoon, but no matter what he says, I want to go. Even if it means you have to give me CPR." He bit his lip and the laugh disappeared. "Look, I almost died, and I'm going to take better care of myself, but I'm not going to sit in an old man's recliner. I'm going to start spending more time with the people I care about." He gave Jake a long look. "That includes you."

Jake nodded. "Okay, if you say so, but be sure you tell him I'll be doing all the lifting and loading. You can supervise." He poked a forefinger at Dale for emphasis. "And let me know this afternoon what he says."

Later that day, Dale dropped by the motel after his doctor visit. Jake met him at the front door.

"What did Doc say about the trip?"

"He wasn't too happy about it, but I assured him I'd be on my best behavior and let you do the heavy work. He made me promise to go to the nearest ER if I felt any chest discomfort."

SATURDAY, JUNE 26TH

Early the next morning, they set out for Atlanta. Neither would own up to it, but they were excited about the trip. Jake guided the truck down country roads and small towns until he picked up I-20 at Abilene. As they traveled, they recalled old memories, the things that had bonded them as kids and later as young men in high school. Then they began bringing each other up to date since Jake had left Archer Springs. They stopped for a long lunch in Fort Worth, still talking, before resuming the long drive. As they shared their stories, they came to know each other as men. Some of the things Dale told him were painful for Jake to hear, but he wanted to know everything. He had missed so much in his life.

At one point, Dale asked the question Jake had been waiting for.

"I think I know the answer, but how come you never married? Hasn't it been lonely for you? Wasn't there ever anyone else?"

Jake nodded but kept his eyes on the highway.

"I almost married a couple of times, but in the end, I couldn't go through with it. It wouldn't have been fair to them. They've both married other people since then. I resigned myself to being a bachelor for the rest of my life."

"But that's all behind you now."

Jake turned to look at Dale in the growing darkness. "What do you mean?"

"Marilyn's never stopped loving you. The whole time we were together, it was you she cared about."

Jake felt himself tense inside. He hadn't seen her since the night she'd come to the house asking about his blood type.

"Sorry, Jake. I know that's a sore subject with you. Give it some time. Maybe things will work out."

They didn't avoid the subject of Monty, though. Dale told Jake about Sheridan coercing Monty, and how the younger man admitted he couldn't burn down Jake's house because it had been his childhood hideout.

Jake groaned.

"That kind of talk gives me the willies, knowing my own son used my house as a place to go and think out his problems. It's the same place I used to go when I had a problem, only Aunt Nora was always there for me. The fact neither one of us knew about the other makes it even more amazing."

Dale grinned. "When do you want to meet him?"

Jake gazed out the pickup window.

"Does he have any idea you're not his birth father?"

Dale shook his head. "No. When he was young, we didn't want to upset him. As he got older, we figured we'd wait and see what happened. In hindsight, we should have told him a long time ago."

Jake glanced over at Dale. "How do you feel about your son meeting me? That must be hard for you to deal with. I know it would be for me."

"I have to admit, it's one of the hardest things I'll ever do in my lifetime. If it was anyone else, I wouldn't be too anxious for it to happen. But you and I go back a long way, Jake. And it's been the plan from the beginning—when you came back, you'd have the right to know your son. He's twenty-four years old. I think he can handle it. Of course, we should give him time to recover from the gunshot and his ordeal with Sheridan. What do you think?"

"We'll see. Let's play it by ear. There's been enough pain and stress for all of us for the time being."

Marilyn pulled back the curtains in Monty's hospital room. Sunlight flooded the dim interior. "That's much better."

"Thanks, Mom." Monty sat on the side of the bed, slid his feet into his house shoes, and shuffled his way to a chair in the corner of the room.

"That's great, Monty. You're doing good. I'll be glad when I get you home with me and get some decent food in your stomach. When did Dr. Ashworth say you would be released?"

Monty reached for the orange juice on his meal tray. "I've been wanting to talk to you about that. I think I'll stay at home with Dad when the doctor releases me."

"But, Monty, your dad isn't even at home right now. I told you he went to Atlanta."

Monty frowned. "Yeah, that's kinda strange, isn't it? Him going with that man whose house burned."

Marilyn swallowed and took a deep breath. "It's not so strange. They knew each other in high school. They haven't seen each other in a long time."

"When's he coming back?"

Marilyn shrugged. "Monday or Tuesday, I think."

"Everything's fine then. He'll be back by the time I'm released." Monty took a long drink of the juice and leaned back in the chair. "Besides, if I'm released before then, you know you can stay with me for a few days if you want. Dad won't mind you being there."

Marilyn crossed her arms. "I don't know ..." The day she'd walked in on Dale and Kay in each other's arms, she'd promised herself she wouldn't do anything to jeopardize their relationship. She had taken him away from Kay once before, but she determined not to do it again.

Monty tossed the empty juice container into the waste basket. "Mom, do you know who gave blood for me?"

"Dr. Ashworth said the donor wants to remain anonymous. Why?"

Monty shrugged. "Just wondered."

Marilyn knelt in front of Monty's chair and took his hands in hers.

"We didn't think you were going to live. You'd already lost a lot of blood when Jake—"

"Who's Jake?"

"He found you. He's also the man your dad went to Atlanta with."

"Did he see what happened?"

"I don't think so. He found you in the alley. When I think what might have happened if he hadn't been there ..." She blinked back tears.

"Don't cry, Mom. The important thing is he found me. I want to meet him so I can thank him. Can you get him to come up here?"

CHAPTER 27

Mr. Woods insisted Jake move into the living quarters he had occupied most of his life.

"We don't need to do that right now," Jake said.

Mr. Woods shook his head.

"You've got a trailer load of furniture sitting outside. You need to get it moved in and settle down to your new position. I've already got my room picked out, actually two rooms joined by a door. One of the rooms can be my living room and the other my bedroom. It will be plenty for me."

Jake helped him move into his new quarters. When they finished, Mr. Woods looked around. "This is perfect. Lots of space to sleep and hang my hat."

Jake placed a leather recliner in front of the television.

"It goes without saying that this is still your home as long as you're here. You don't need to change anything you've been doing in the kitchen or anywhere else all these years, except that you can relax from running the place."

Kay and Dale arrived soon after with a basket of muffins, fresh flowers, and a new tablecloth.

Jake grinned. "And to what do I owe this honor?"

Kay shook out the tablecloth.

"Housewarming celebration. We wanted to be the first to welcome back Archer Springs's newest resident businessman."

"Thank you." He poured coffee for the three of them while Dale reached for a blueberry muffin.

"This is like old times."

Jake sipped the steaming brew. He agreed except for one thing. One of them was missing from the group.

The man from Archer Springs Air and Heat arrived while they were talking.

Kay laughed. "I see you're making improvements already."

"I'm used to central air. I think the customers will appreciate it too."

Dale and Kay left after the muffins and coffee were gone, and Jake started painting Mr. Woods's former living quarters. Later that day, when he moved his furniture in, he felt as though he'd returned from a long journey. The motel felt more like home than any of the pricey apartments he'd rented in Atlanta.

Marilyn watched Dale and Monty search for the TV remote. She and Kay had tidied up the place while Dale and Jake were gone, but you couldn't tell it now. Father and son had wreaked havoc on the place.

"Are you two sure you're going to be okay?"

"Mom, quit making a fuss. Dad and I have lived alone for five years." Monty walked over and put his arm around her. "Relax. We'll be fine."

Dale retrieved an empty paper plate from the coffee table.

"He's right, you know."

She sighed. "I know, but you've both been in the hospital."

Dale found the remote under a stack of newspapers and collapsed into the recliner. He smirked.

"I'm not such a bad cook. And Myra Crandell still comes once a week to clean."

Marilyn shrugged. "I know, but ..."

Kay took the crumpled paper plate from Dale and picked up an empty glass. "Marilyn, if you're worried about them, why don't you stay at my house a few more days? You can be here in five minutes if anything happens."

Dale shook his head at the two of them. "She can stay here with me and Monty if she's that worried about us." He glanced at Marilyn. "It was your home for years."

Marilyn frowned. "I'll stay with Kay, but if you need me, you'd better call. I mean it."

"We will, Mom. Promise." Monty gave her a quick peck on the cheek. "I'm starved. Want something, Dad?"

Dale frowned. "Doc says no more junk food for me. I have to eat healthy now."

Kay located her purse. "I've got errands to run. I'll see you at the house, Marilyn."

After the door closed behind Kay, Dale turned to Marilyn. "We need to talk. Let's go out on the front porch."

She followed him out and chose a wicker chair. "What is it?"

Dale leaned against the porch rail. "I wanted to talk to you about Jake and Monty. Remember our plan when we eloped?"

Marilyn nodded. She'd known this conversation was coming.

Dale cleared his throat. "Now that Jake has moved here, I think he and Monty should meet. They have the right to know each other." He paused. "Jake is a little uncertain about it, says he doesn't want to upset Monty. I think Monty can handle it."

Marilyn stared out across the yard. She wasn't ready to hand Monty over to Jake as though nothing had happened. The pain had been too great. Besides, Jake had made no effort to resume their relationship.

"Marilyn, you know I wouldn't say anything to hurt you, don't you?"

She reined in her thoughts and forced herself to face Dale. "I know." She traced the pattern on the chair arm with one finger.

"I think," Dale said slowly, "the reason Jake is hesitant about Monty has something to do with you."

"Why do you think that?" Her eyes were steady on him.

"There's no other reason why he shouldn't meet his own son. I don't think Jake will push the situation unless he knows you approve."

Her voice trembled. "I don't want Monty hurt the way we were."

Dale shook his head. "Why would he hurt Monty? Jake's suffered as much as we have, maybe more. After all, we had everything"—Dale waved his arm toward the town—"our friends, home, family, a son. Jake was left with nothing."

Dale paced to the far end of the porch and then back to stand in front of her.

"Do something for me. Go to Jake and tell him you think he should meet Monty. Give our son a chance to know the father who gave him life, and then saved that same life twenty-five years later."

Marilyn nodded slowly. "Okay. For Monty's sake, I'll go see Jake."

It would take every remaining shred of her pride just to face him.

Tuesday, June 29th, 4:00 p.m.

"Hi, Jake."

Jake looked up from his newspaper. "Hello, Billy. I didn't hear you come in."

"You were lost in that newspaper," the deputy said. "I don't think a tornado could've gotten your attention."

Jake folded the newspaper and tossed it on the coffee table. "What's on your mind?"

Billy sat and propped one boot on the top of his knee.

"Thought you might like to know. We have a confession from one of Sheridan's cronies. He may be going away for a long time."

"What did you find out? Or is it confidential?"

"The newspaper's going to run it, so I guess I can tell you, but keep it under your hat until word gets out." He leaned forward and lowered his voice. "It seems Sheridan discovered natural gas underneath the town."

Jake whistled under his breath. "No wonder he wanted all that property, along with all those mineral rights. He'd be sitting on a fortune. "

"Well, not anymore." Billy tasted his coffee, then set the cup on the table. "Sheriff Abel's ready to throw the book at him. He says all the property Sheridan cheated people out of should be returned to the original owners. They're entitled to the royalties." Billy grinned. "Sheridan's sitting in his cell, crying the blues."

"Serves him right. Some prison time might scare the greed right out of him."

CHAPTER 28

THURSDAY, JULY 1ST, 8:00 P.M.

Jake walked out on the porch and stretched. The night had arrived, all quiet and peaceful. At the edge of the empty street, he looked up. Stars like sky jewels twinkled a greeting. A cricket serenaded the evening from somewhere in the darkness.

Reynolds, you made a smart decision when you decided to stay here.

He'd enjoyed every hectic moment since the day Mr. Woods had signed the motel over to him. Business had been brisk this vacation season. Most visitors were one-nighters on their way to elsewhere, but they were paying customers. He couldn't complain. And Dale came every morning for coffee. Jake could almost set his clock by the silver Ford truck pulling up in front of the motel.

Jake examined the night sky another moment, then headed inside when a noise made him turn back toward the street. He didn't recognize the car. But he absolutely knew the driver as soon as she opened the door and stepped out.

Marilyn climbed the three steps leading to the motel before she spoke.

"Jake, do you have a few minutes? I'd like to talk to you."

"Sure. Come inside where it's cooler." Her perfume floated out to greet him as she walked past. A butterfly flittered in his stomach.

"Would you like some iced tea or a soft drink?" His heart seemed out of rhythm. He needed something to do with his hands.

"No, thank you. I'm fine."

She perched on the edge of the sofa. Her lips and nails were tinted a luscious shade of pink, and he longed to run his fingers through that silky hair. He struggled to breathe.

"Dale said he explained everything to you about our marriage—and about Monty." She looked at the floor, not meeting his eyes.

"Yes." An overwhelming sense of what she'd suffered swept through him. "Marilyn, I'm really sorry." He swallowed hard. "You don't know how sorry I am for everything."

She ignored his apology. "Would you like to meet Monty?"

"Only if you think it's a good idea." He leaned against the desk for support. "I don't want to cause trouble."

"He wants to meet the man who saved his life."

"He knows who I am?"

Marilyn shook her head, keeping her eyes averted. "No, we haven't told him."

Jake relaxed as though a weight was off his shoulders.

"I didn't do anything remarkable. Any decent person would have done the same thing."

"You saved his life." She met his gaze for the first time since she'd come in. "And you were his blood donor too, yes?"

Jake sighed and nodded.

"But that day at your house, I didn't know if you'd help us or not."

Jake felt as though a knife had plunged into his heart. "Marilyn, I'm sorry about the way I acted that day. That was before—"

He stopped, went to the chair next to where she sat on the sofa, and sat next to her. He reached for her hand, but when she flinched, he withdrew his hand and looked at the floor.

"I couldn't imagine why you would come to me after all these years and ask me to donate blood to your son, after everything that happened to us."

"I had no choice twenty-five years ago, nor did I have a choice the day I came to see you. Monty was dying."

Jake intertwined his fingers to stop their trembling.

"I had so much anger bottled up inside. I never stopped to think there might be a rational reason for the two of you marrying." He unclasped his hands and ran them through his hair. "How could I have known?"

A muffled sob escaped her.

Jake's head jerked up. Her eyes shone with unshed tears. He wanted to wrap her in his arms and shut out the memory of those lost years. He begged her with his eyes to understand. He saw her swallow and thought she might speak, but she didn't.

"It wasn't until later I learned you'd had a son nine months after I left town and named him after my grandfather."

Marilyn wiped her eyes. "What about my letter? Didn't you read it?"

Jake shook his head. "I got the letter, but I didn't read it. I couldn't. I was too angry."

"So you never knew the reason we married was because of the baby."

Jake shook his head. "I only found out a couple of days ago. Someone in town knew, and he's been hinting like crazy since I got here."

The color drained from Marilyn's face. "Who was it?"

"Carl Malone."

Marilyn's jaw dropped.

"He overheard you and Dale talking in his parking lot the night you told Dale you were pregnant. He never told anyone, but from the moment I arrived here, he's pushed me to go see Dale and make things right." Jake cleared his throat. "He insisted I check out the birth records from 1958, so I went to the courthouse and checked Monty's birth record. From there, I went back to Malone, and he verified everything. That's what made me decide to go see Dale. I wanted to hear it from his mouth."

Marilyn met his gaze. "We didn't know what else to do. You were gone, and Daddy wanted me to have an abortion." She hesitated, her voice cracking with emotion. "I couldn't let him kill our baby, Jake." Tears spilled over and rolled down her cheeks.

His heart knotted. His lack of self-control had caused this pain. He reached out and covered her hands with his, and this time she didn't flinch.

"It's okay," he said. "I know you were only trying to protect our child." He took a deep breath. "I owe you an apology."

"No, you don't."

"Yes, I do. It's my fault everything turned out as it did. I should have been stronger." He looked her full in the face. "Will you forgive me?"

Marilyn nodded, wiping at the tears on her cheeks.

He stood and pulled her into his arms, but she pulled away and started for the door.

"Marilyn, wait. Where are you going?"

She stopped, hand on the door frame, and shook her head.

"I'm glad we all know the truth of the matter now, but too much time has passed. Dale asked me to come and talk with you about Monty, and I did. Now maybe we should leave well enough alone." She pushed open the door and stepped outside.

Jake felt numb all over. She wanted nothing to do with him. He hurried to the door as her car pulled away from the motel. He ran into the street and jogged alongside the car window.

"Marilyn, please. Wait."

In the glow of the streetlamps, he could see her face through the car window. When she turned her head to look at him, the pain in her eyes stood out like a glow-in-the-dark image. She gunned the engine and drove away. He stayed outside, watching her taillights shrink to faint red dots in the distance.

CHAPTER 29

Marilyn vowed to stay away from Jake. They'd both suffered, and she didn't know if it was possible to forget all the pain. The next morning, she called Dale, told him about her meeting with Jake, and then, she packed her suitcase to head home.

Kay stood in the doorway watching. "You know you don't have to leave. I thought you wanted to keep an eye on them."

Marilyn tried to act lighthearted. "It's time I checked on my houseplants. They're wilted by now." She looked at Kay. "Will you watch them for me?"

"Of course. No need to even ask."

Marilyn carried her suitcase out to the car, with Kay following her.

"I'm going to miss you. It's been like old times, having you and Jake both here."

Marilyn stowed her luggage in the trunk, then hugged Kay.

"Take care of yourself and Dale. The two of you deserve some happiness."

She stepped into her car, started the engine, and waved goodbye. As she left Archer Springs in her rearview mirror, she glanced back only once, her heart like a weight in her chest. She was leaving behind everything and everyone that mattered to her.

SATURDAY, JULY 3RD

The morning after Marilyn's departure, Dale brought Monty to the motel. Jake almost didn't recognize him in his jeans and boots, clean-shaven and with a haircut. Jake wondered if the change had been Monty's idea or Dale's.

Dale's grin stretched ear-to-ear. "Monty, I want you to meet my oldest friend in the world, Jake Reynolds. He's also the man who rescued you."

Monty extended his hand. "Mr. Reynolds, I don't know how to thank you for what you did."

Jake shook the offered hand.

"No thanks necessary. Good to meet you, Monty."

Minus the ponytail, Monty looked like a twenty-four-year-old mirror image of Jake, with eyes the same shade of blue. Jake had a sudden urge to grab the young man and hug him.

Dale placed a hand on each of their shoulders. "Something else you don't know, Son. Jake saved your bacon twice. He's the one who donated blood for you."

Monty's eyes widened, and he looked as though he might cry.

"Thank you again, then, Mr. Reynolds."

Jake poured coffee for the three of them, to let everyone's emotions simmer down.

"If you guys are such old friends," Monty said, after he'd sipped on his coffee, "how come I haven't heard about it before? Like stories about the old days?"

Dale poked Monty's arm. "Old days? Watch it, kid."

Jake winked at Monty. "Did Dale ever tell you about the time he got caught stealing watermelons?" When Monty shook his head, Jake proceeded to tell the story, while Dale alternately filled in bits of information and good-naturedly objected to Jake's embellishments.

They laughed and talked like they were at a family reunion, until Jake mentioned Aunt Nora's house.

Monty stared at Jake, the color draining from his face. "*You* owned the big old house on Orchard Street?"

Jake nodded. He looked at Dale for support.

Dale winked in reply. "Go ahead," he said. "Tell him."

Monty looked from one to the other. "Tell me what?"

Jake set his cup on the table.

"The house belonged to my aunt and uncle. I inherited it from them. When I was a kid, I used to go there all the time when I had a problem to work out." He glanced up at Monty. "Your dad tells me you did the same thing."

Monty nodded, his face turning deep red. "Excuse me."

He stood and walked out the door, and Jake looked at Dale.

"What did I say wrong?"

Dale shook his head. "He's just embarrassed. Go talk to him. I'll wait in here."

Jake found Monty on the bench outside the door. He sat on the opposite end.

"Monty, there's nothing to be embarrassed about. I know all about Sheridan."

Monty wrung his hands. "But you don't understand. I almost set your house on fire." His voice cracked with emotion. "If I hadn't seen you standing on the porch that day, I might've done it, but I got scared. And that's not all." He stared at his shoes.

"I'm the one who made the anonymous phone call to scare you out of town. And I sprayed your walls with red paint." He looked at Jake and shook his head. "And after everything I did to you, you still helped me."

Jake could see guilt and misery written all over his son's face. He knew those feelings well.

"Look, we all do things that make us ashamed afterwards. At the time, we're positive we're not doing anything bad. It's only after the damage is done that we realize our mistakes."

He reached over and placed his hand on Monty's shoulder. "All is forgiven, okay? We didn't know about Sheridan's spider web then. He caused all of us grief. I'm just glad I was in the alley the night you were shot and able to give blood when you needed it."

Monty looked at Jake but didn't speak. Jake patted him on the back. "What do you say we go get more coffee and doughnuts before your dad finishes them off? The doctor'll raise sand with him big-time if we don't rescue him from himself."

CHAPTER 30

MONDAY, JULY 12TH

A bond developed between Jake and Monty, but Jake was careful not to come between Dale and the boy he'd raised from birth. Twice, Jake had almost slipped and called him *Son*. He dreaded the day he'd make that mistake and have to explain himself.

On a sweltering July Monday afternoon, Monty came to the motel lobby alone. Jake glanced up from his paperwork.

"Hey, I didn't hear you come in. How're you doing?"

"I have to talk to you."

Jake laid down his ballpoint pen and leaned back in his chair. He hoped his pounding pulse wasn't visible over his collar.

"Okay. Have a seat and let's talk."

Monty sat. "You're more than my dad's buddy from high school, aren't you?"

His tone was almost accusatory. Jake searched for the right words.

"We were like brothers growing up." He didn't want to lie, but the look in those blue eyes demanded an answer. Jake sat back in his chair. "Why don't you tell me what's really bothering you?"

Monty popped his knuckles. "When I went in for my checkup yesterday, I asked Dr. Ashworth about having a rare blood type, and about you having the same. He told me he's never met anyone else with AB negative before, and yet there's two of us here in Archer Springs."

"If you remember, I was here on a visit to see about the house. I lived in Atlanta, not here." Jake stopped. Maybe it was best to just let Monty talk until he got everything off his chest.

Monty rubbed his eyes as if he'd stayed up all night worrying about the situation.

"And this thing about your house. Doesn't it give you the creeps, knowing we both spent time there?"

"It is kind of strange."

Monty scratched his head. "And after I shaved off my beard and cut my hair, we kind of looked alike, I thought." He raised his hands and let them fall into his lap. "We even eat the same kinds of food. It's like we're on the same wavelength."

He exhaled, frustration clear on his face.

"Yesterday I was in the attic poking around and found these." He pulled some snapshots from his shirt pocket and tossed them on the counter. "I've never seen these before." He stared hard at Jake for a moment.

Jake felt nervous perspiration trickle down the side of his face, but remained silent.

Monty popped his knuckles again and picked up one of the snapshots. "I found this picture of you and my dad together with his '57 Chevy. I've heard him talk about that car all my life, yet he never mentioned you." He licked his lips. "But the picture I wondered about most was this one." He reached for another photo and held it out to Jake.

Jake remembered the day they had posed for that shot in front of Brown's Drug Store. It was a few weeks before high school graduation, and Mr. Brown had done the honors and snapped the picture with Marilyn's camera. Jake remembered stepping behind Marilyn and wrapping his arms around her waist, while she leaned back against him, resting her head on his shoulder. Dale stood next to Kay, his arm draped across her shoulder.

Jake cleared his throat. "I remember the day this was taken."

Monty seemed to have forgotten the photo for the moment. He spoke with emotion, as if he was fighting tears. "And then you saved my life, after everything I tried to do to you. I could have killed you, but you called the ambulance and then donated blood to me, even though I didn't deserve it."

Jake reached out and touched Monty's shoulder.

"In the past few weeks, I've learned some things about my own past that I'm not too proud of either. None of us are perfect. We all need forgiveness, even when we think we don't deserve it." He squeezed Monty's arm. "It's something my aunt used to talk about all the time. It's called grace."

Monty shook his head. "I hear what you're saying, but it still doesn't make sense."

Jake shrugged. "I don't understand it either. I'm having to get used to grace myself." He tried to smile, but an uneasy feeling crept over him. This wasn't how he'd imagined doing this. He rubbed the back of his neck and felt the gold chain he had put on when he dressed that morning. *Marilyn.*

He realized Monty had quit talking and was waiting for him to say something. He said the only thing that came to mind.

"Okay, what do you make of all this?"

Monty rubbed perspiration from his face. He paced back and forth across the room, then came back to stand in front of Jake, pale-faced and trembling.

"I don't know too many people who would help someone who tried to kill them." He swallowed hard. "But a father would. A father would do anything for his kid."

He took a deep, shuddering breath. "Are you—" Monty's eyes brimmed with tears, and Jake nodded.

"I'm your father, yes."

Monty gulped and sniffed. "But how—" He stopped, confusion written across his face. "I mean, why? Where have you been all this time? How come you never showed up before now?" Monty closed his eyes as if to stop the questions. He pounded the palm of his hand with his other fist and then opened his eyes and looked at Jake.

"Dad never said anything, never gave any hint he wasn't my real father."

Jake heard the turmoil in Monty's voice. He knew the feeling all too well. He'd wondered so many times about the betrayal he was sure had been perpetrated against him. His heart went out to his son, and he put his arm around Monty.

"Dale is a special person. Why don't we sit down? It's a long story, and you'll want to hear it all."

CHAPTER 31

MONDAY, AUGUST 2ND, 5:00 P.M.

Monty came by more often after learning the details of his parents' past. Jake worried Dale might begin to feel left out. One Monday afternoon in the first week of August when Dale came by alone, Jake questioned him about it, but Dale just chuckled and slapped him on the back.

"You worry too much. Monty and I have a strong relationship. He still calls me Dad, and I won't object if he calls you the same." He shook his head. "I'll admit it's been hard to get to this point, but it was always the plan if you ever came home." He gently punched Jake's upper arm. "I've never had another friend like you. We've always shared everything since we were kids."

Jake grinned and nodded. "Even your '57 Chevy."

"Well, Monty's carrying on that tradition. After all, he is your son."

Even though Jake had enjoyed every minute of getting to know Monty and running the motel, an emptiness remained inside him. Four weeks had passed since the night Marilyn had come to the motel, and he ached to see her again. The smoldering coals he'd thought long dead had burst back into life.

He'd thought of calling her, even dialed her number a couple of times, but his pride hung up the phone before she answered. He'd considered driving to her house and knocking on the door, but the possibility of rejection stopped him.

That same evening of his conversation with Dale, Jake grilled hamburgers for Monty and Dale, Billy, Carl Malone, and Jonathan Woods. Small talk and a lot of laughter among the men floated across the warm Texas evening. He couldn't remember the last time he had enjoyed himself this much, just cooking and talking, enjoying the camaraderie. He felt as if he had been given a second chance at life.

Soon after they finished eating, Jonathan Woods and Carl Malone left to play dominoes at the VFW hall. Dale and Monty left a few minutes later to go home. Billy departed soon after that to go on duty at the sheriff's department.

After they were all gone, the quiet emptiness left Jake lonely and bored. He paced the lobby in frustration. Desperate for something to do, he dug out Aunt Nora's treasure chest and began going through the contents, until the old 45s caught his attention.

He retrieved the ancient record player Mr. Woods had given him. After a little fiddling to get the vinyl records to fit the spindle, he stacked the 45s on the player and switched it on. The first record dropped, and the familiar melody of "Only You" filled the room.

Jake turned off the motel porch light and went outside to sit in the dark. He closed his eyes and let the music roll over him, wishing Marilyn was here to share the mood with him.

MONDAY, AUGUST 2ND, 9:00 P.M.

Marilyn slowed the car as she reached the city limits of Archer Springs. No one knew she was coming. She hadn't known herself until three hours ago, when she couldn't stand being alone any longer.

The past few weeks had been an empty existence. Thoughts of Jake had tormented her. She knew she only had two choices—live out the rest of her days alone, or swallow her pride and let him back into her life.

At the solitary stop light, Marilyn turned east toward the town square. When the motel came into view, she noticed the lack of activity—no lights burning except for the neon VACANCY sign. Everyone had apparently turned in for the night.

Now what? Go back home? Ring the bell? Tell him I need a room for the night? Ha! That would be really ironic.

She parked on the opposite side of the street and slid out. The faint sound of music floated through the air, and she leaned against the car door to listen. Her heart almost stopped beating. It was their song, hers and Jake's. The smooth, mellow voices of The Platters drifted out to her, intensifying her loneliness.

The music came from the direction of the motel, and Marilyn started across the street. The closer she got to the motel, the louder the music became. Jake was playing their song. *Did that mean he was thinking about her?* She increased her pace.

Marilyn didn't notice the man sitting in the darkness on the front porch bench until he spoke.

"Marilyn?"

She had to restrain herself from running to him, acting like a fool.

"Where did you find that music?"

"In Aunt Nora's treasure chest." He paused. "Come sit down. We can listen together." He made room for her on the bench. She took a deep breath and sat on the edge.

They listened in silence for a time as the music played. Marilyn couldn't see the details of his face, but she could feel his body heat mixing with hers in the small space between them. The air hummed with emotion. That old familiar feeling, the one she felt only when she was with Jake, was still there.

When the song ended, he stood. "Be right back." He returned seconds later. "Sorry. had to re-start the music." He held out his hand. "Would you dance with me?"

Marilyn stood, and Jake slipped his arms around her. She wondered if he could hear her pounding heart. Together they glided up and down the motel porch, lost in the music and each other, until the song ended.

When the song ended, Jake looked down at Marilyn.

"I'm sorry I broke my promise to you. Sorry I didn't come back sooner."

"I assumed you read my letter and knew I'd married Dale."

"I did know, because Kay wrote me right after it happened. She didn't want me to come back without knowing." He looked away for a moment. "I just didn't know the rest of it."

Marilyn sighed. "You can't imagine what it was like all those years, married to one man and in love with another."

A warm sensation spread through his body. "Are you saying you still love me?"

"I've never stopped." She leaned her head against his chest. "I promised I'd wait for you. In a way, I guess I still am."

His voice dropped low, almost a whisper.

"I'm here now. Am I too late?"

Marilyn raised her head to look him full in the face. "It's never too late to love the right person."

Jake lowered his lips to hers and kissed her. This time she didn't resist. The years of bitterness and separation evaporated. Afterwards, he held her close for several minutes, then released her. "I have something for you."

Jake lifted the chain from around his neck and held it up. It sparkled and glittered in the dim light from a nearby streetlamp.

Marilyn gasped. "Where did you get that?"

"Something else Aunt Nora saved for us." Jake slipped it around her neck, then drew her into his arms again. He chuckled. "You know, she spoke to me after I arrived here."

Marilyn pulled back and looked at him. "What do you mean she spoke to you?" She shivered. "That's creepy. She's been gone over twenty years."

Jake nodded. "I went to the cemetery not long after I got to town. You know what's written on her tombstone?" He didn't wait for Marilyn to answer. "'For if ye forgive men their trespasses, your heavenly Father will also forgive you. But if ye forgive not men their trespasses, neither will your Father forgive your trespasses.'"

"That sounds like something your Aunt Nora would say."

He laughed. "Well, she's not the original author. God is. But you know what I think? I think she put it on her tombstone for me, hoping I would come back some day and see it. She wanted to be sure I did the right thing."

Marilyn touched his lips with her fingertip. "That *we* did the right thing."

"Yes. We all thought we were doing the right thing."

Marilyn leaned against him. "I've missed you so much all these years. No matter how hard I tried, I couldn't get you out of my heart."

"And I couldn't get you out of mine. Our two hearts belonged together."

She twisted to look at his face.

"Has there ever been anyone else for you, Jake?"

He gently turned her head to rest on his shoulder again, and kept his hand against her hair. He held her tighter and smiled at the stars spying on them from overhead.

"Only you, Marilyn," he said softly. "Only you."

ABOUT THE AUTHOR

Vickie Phelps has been writing since 1988. She is the author or coauthor of twelve books. Her five novels include *Postmark From the Past, Wheels of Justice, Moved, Left No Address, Waiting for Joy,* and *A Christmas Legacy.* Nonfiction works include *Psalms for the Common Man, Gratitude: The Art of Being Thankful, (gift book), The 5-Minute Prayer Plan for Women,* and *10 Things to Remember When Times Are Bad.* She is coauthor with Jo Huddleston of *Writing101: A Handbook of Tips and Encouragement for Writers* and *Simply Christmas: Memories, Traditions, and Stories of the Season.* Vickie is coauthor with Emily Biggers of *Mornings with God: My Daily Prayer Journal.*

365 Treasured Moments for Mothers & Daughters, a perpetual calendar, was released by Barbour Publishing in 2007.

A series of small gift books was published by Barbour Publishing for their Daymaker line. *Simple Pleasures,* (2004); *Star of Wonder,* (2003); *101 Things to be Thankful for,*

(2003); *May Christ be the Center of Your Christmas*, (2001); *101 Keys for Life*, (2000). *101 Keys for Life* made the Christian Booksellers Bestseller List for gift books in 2000.

Vickie's work is included in several anthologies including, *The Best of the Proverbs 31 Ministry from The Proverbs 31 Ministry, Seasons of a Woman's Heart* from Starburst Publishers, *The Writers' Journal Guide to the Writing Life*, from Writers' Journal Books, *A Cup of Comfort Cookbook* from Adams Media, *For Better or Worse* from Christian Publications, Inc., *God's Little Rule Book* from Starburst Publishers, and *A Treasure Box*, a publication of the Northeast Texas Writers Organization from Pennant publishing.

Over 200 articles have been published in publications such as *Woman's Touch, Lutheran Woman Today, Christian Education Counselor, Church of God Evangel, Christian Standard, Mature Living, Longview News Journal, Evangel, The War Cry, Lutheran Journal, The Dollar Stretcher, and CBN.com*.

Vickie lives in East Texas with her husband, William Phelps (Sonny). They attend Calvary Assembly of God in Henderson where Vickie fills in as organist, teaches Sunday school, and edits the weekly church bulletin.

Vickie is the founder and former director of East Texas Christian Writers Group in Longview, Texas. She worked for eighteen years as a bookseller for an independent bookstore, six of those years as buyer for the store. She retired from the store in 2012.

www.ingramcontent.com/pod-product-compliance
Lightning Source LLC
Chambersburg PA
CBHW070053260626
47160CB00004B/1196